20 Greatest Political Philosophers

Kalyani Mookherji is an alumnus of Jadavpur University, Kolkata, from where she finished her post-graduation in English Literature. She has been a writer and educator for over ten years now. She also runs a popular literary workshop for children, Feeling Bookerish, in Wellington, a town in The Nilgiris District of Tamil Nadu, where she currently resides after having travelled the length and breadth of India as an army wife.

Despite being a busy mom to a bright teen and a spoilt dog, she finds time for her other interests such as music, baking and blogging at crumbsonmynotebook.wordpress.com. Previously, she has written *100 Greatest Sportspersons*.

20 Greatest Political Philosophers

KALYANI MOOKHERJI

Published by
Rupa Publications India Pvt. Ltd 2019
7/16, Ansari Road, Daryaganj
New Delhi 110002

Sales centres:

Allahabad Bengaluru Chennai
Hyderabad Jaipur Kathmandu
Kolkata Mumbai

Copyright © Kalyani Mookherji 2019

The views and opinions expressed in this book are the author's
own and the facts are as reported by her which have been
verified to the extent possible, and the publishers are not
in any way liable for the same

All rights reserved.
No part of this publication may be reproduced, transmitted,
or stored in a retrieval system, in any form or by any means,
electronic, mechanical, photocopying, recording or otherwise,
without the prior permission of the publisher.

ISBN: 978-93-5333-374-4

First impression 2019

10 9 8 7 6 5 4 3 2 1

Printed at HT Media Ltd, Gr. Noida

This book is sold subject to the condition that it shall not,
by way of trade or otherwise, be lent, resold, hired out, or otherwise circulated,
without the publisher's prior consent, in any form of binding or cover other than
that in which it is published.

CONTENTS

Introduction	vii
1. Confucius	1
2. Plato	9
3. Aristotle	17
4. Kautilya	24
5. Al-Farabi	29
6. Maimonides	36
7. Thiruvalluvar	43
8. Niccolò Machiavelli	48
9. Thomas Hobbes	55
10. John Locke	62
11. Montesquieu	69
12. Jean-Jacques Rousseau	79
13. Edmund Burke	87
14. Immanuel Kant	94
15. Mary Wollstonecraft	101

16. Thomas Jefferson — 111
17. John Stuart Mill — 120
18. Tocqueville — 128
19. Karl Marx — 136
20. Michel Foucault — 144

Conclusion: New Directions — 153

INTRODUCTION

What makes the human society different from 'groups' formed by other species? After all, ants have their colonies, bees have their hives and wolves their packs—all marked by a distinct hierarchy and in some cases, even division of labour. Different thinkers have found different answers to this most fundamental of question—for some, it is the concept of virtuous living while for others, it is the use of reason that separates the social life of mankind from even their nearest animal cousins.

The earliest humans came together to live in a group when they discovered that strength lies in numbers—they reasoned that chances of surviving an animal attack or hunting for food increased considerably when done as a team. However, as the species thrived and the groups became larger, there was a need for everyone to agree on certain rules for the smooth functioning of daily affairs like preservation of property, prevention of theft as well as in case of intermittent events like attacks from other groups or coping with natural disaster. Over time, with newer technology and more effective modes of economic production, such social groups grew in size and complexity, leading to the formation of villages, burgs and cities. Many such groups emerged in a single geographical region and the most powerful among such groups set out and brought neighbouring ones under its control, leading to the emergence of a state and a ruler.

The word 'political' originates from the Greek word 'polis', literally meaning a city state, implying civic society. Political philosophy thus looks for the underlying principles that human beings apply in organizing their social group in order to lead a harmonious civic life. It often begins with the question about what should be a person's relationship to society and then goes on to consider various political, legal, economic and social systems and institutions that make for the most productive civic existence.

Various theorists have gone on to further refine this field of study, depending on the dominant philosophical orientation of their age—thus the relation between ethics and political philosophy, the separation of moral and political concerns, the differentiation between political philosophy and political science as well as the limits of state power are among some of the directions that thinkers have explored down the ages.

This book takes as its subject twenty philosophers whose theories on the emergence of laws, governance political systems in human society have had the greatest impact on the study of such matters. Among these twenty names, arranged chronologically by date of birth, fifteen are European—the reason for this majority being that their writings have survived and remained popular. Colonialism—economic, political and cultural—had led to the supremacy of the master's languages and texts over those that they controlled. Thus French, Spanish and English became the new international languages of production and dissemination of knowledge from seventeenth century onwards. Even in regions with long and rich histories of complex political systems like China, India, West Asia, their treatises had to be translated into Latin or English for them to become popular on a global scale – the primary reason as to why they have not been as accessible and mainstream as their European counterparts.

The other reason for the dominance of European philosophers was the spread of political liberalism from Europe to other continents, starting with the American War of Independence, the liberal revolutions in South America, the reform movements like the 'Al-Nahda' and 'Tanzimat' in West Asia, but more markedly in the twentieth century when colonized nations like India used the writings of Locke, Rousseau, Jefferson to demand political independence. Indeed, many nations including Haiti and India based their constitutions on the writings of these European philosophers. Many new democracies adopted features like the party system, the two-house legislature as well as others like separation of powers of religious and political authority and so on. These markers of modern civil society would draw most extensively from European political philosophers – even though many of them had actually been supporters of colonialism and even slavery – which is why they came to dominate mainstream political theory.

The second glaring attribute of these twenty names is the dominance of male thinkers—the only woman who figures in this book is Mary Wollstonecraft. The absence of women in the history of political philosophy has largely been the result of the historical patriarchal distinction between the private and public sphere, where women have always been restricted to the former. Though Plato concedes that women too can become philosophers in his ideal *Republic*, not much is heard about actual women figures taking active part in governance or political life in ancient Greece. The island of Lesbos and the land of Amazons belong to the realm of mythology while anthropologists have still not come across historical records with primary sources on any purely matriarchal society – where women hold political, legal, economic and cultural power – or gynocratic society which means 'rule by women'.

Undoubtedly, there have been famous women names in ruling politics – ranging from female pharaohs and empresses to regents and spiritual leaders – but very few wrote theories about polity and governance. That is not to indicate that women never wrote about public matters—rather that their writings were largely pushed to the sidelines. Thus, the nineteenth century Italian noblewoman, Maria Marchesa Florenzi, found her works banned by the Church as heretical while, even in the twentieth century, political journalist and communist activist, Anna Louise Strong, was forced to leave her own country for Russia and later China where she died. Also, women writing about politics often chose to focus on practical matters and experiences like the need for educational reform or extension of voting rights rather than theoretical principles of polity.

To sum it up, it was the cumulative effect of centuries of patriarchy which kept women from becoming a dominant presence in the public domain—whether in legislature where laws are made, actual governance where laws are implemented or the academia where theories are perpetuated. Not surprisingly, as late as 2011, the UN General Assembly's resolution on women's political participation noted that, 'Women in every part of the world continue to be largely marginalized from the political sphere, often as a result of discriminatory laws, practices, attitudes and gender stereotypes, low levels of education, lack of access to health care and the disproportionate effect of poverty on women.'

However, with the growing sophistication of political theories addressing questions posed by feminism, post-colonialism, neo-imperialism and environmentalism, as well as societies realizing the benefits of women joining political, educational and religious institutions in larger numbers, now there are more women writing about both the theoretical and practical aspects of polity and governance.

So, here are twenty of the greatest political philosophers ranging from classical to twentieth century, from Western Europe to West and East Asia. These are the names whose theories and thoughts have had the maximum influence on the political and legal institutions of the modern world.

1

CONFUCIUS

Confucius was an ancient Chinese teacher, philosopher and political thinker whose ethical precepts formed the basis of human action, in both private and public lives, during a time of ideological tumult in China. The social and political philosophy based on his teachings came to be known as Confucianism, which, apart from a brief period of Legalism in the second century BCE, held sway in China till the end of the nineteenth century.

EARLY LIFE

Confucius is believed to have been born around 551 BCE in Qifu in the Chinese province of Shandong. Little is known about his early life except that while growing up, the decline of the Zhou dynasty and the accompanying ideological ferment impacted Confucius deeply. He saw the long-held moral and social order breaking down all around him and felt a need for ideas that would make for ethical living, both in the private and public lives of his countrymen.

During his lifetime, Confucius went by other names as Kong Qui or K'ung Fu-tzu. His teachings exist in the 'Four Books' of Confucianism that Chinese philosopher and later disciple, Zhu Xi, published in 1190. The most important of these books is *Lunyu*, which was brought out by Xi as *Sushu* and was eventually translated into English as *Analects of Confucius*. He is also believed to have authored a rearrangement of the *Book of Odes* and revised the historical *Book of Documents*. A historical account of the twelve dukes of Lu, called the *Spring and Autumn Annals* is again believed to have been written by Confucius.

POLITICAL PHILOSOPHY

In response to the changing moral and social codes of his time, Confucius stressed on ethical living. Human beings needed to lead a virtuous life based on self-discipline as well as the principle of loving others or 'ren' or the tender virtue of human feelings. It could be practised by remembering the 'golden rule' understood simply as, 'What you do not wish for yourself, do not do to others'.

Confucius' deep concern with ethics also underlined his political philosophy. According to him, an ideal leader should lead a virtuous life so that his followers and the citizens of the country can emulate his way of living. The hallmark of such virtue was again inner self-discipline, which would protect the leader from falling prey to greed for power, wealth or self-interest. The other main quality of the leader's virtue was compassion for others which would enable him to rule with humility. Such a leader, he believed, would be ideal for all citizens of the country and would even have the potential to make force and punishment unnecessary.

An important aspect of Confucian political tenets dealt with the various ways to cultivate royal 'virtues'. He believed that this could be brought about by the practice of certain ceremonial actions or rituals known as 'li', like sacrificial rites performed at the temple of ancestors, exchange of gifts as well as by acts of courtesy and decorums, like bowing and toasting.

Indeed, Confucius' politics of virtue went much further than visualizing an ideal leader as a morally upright man. According to him, politics, in general, should mean the practice and spread of certain virtues and relationships for the welfare of the entire society. He saw the dangers of a political system which was affected by bribery or coercion and instead, advocated motivating citizens to follow laws based on uniformity in action and virtue.

CONFUCIUS AND LAO TZU

Scholars of political philosophy have often compared Confucius with a slightly older contemporary and another great Chinese philosopher, Lao Tzu—the founder of ancient Chinese philosophy of Taoism which primarily advocated a simple way of life, both in personal and public spheres. Lao Tzu, in Chinese, actually refers to an honorific title meaning, 'Old Master' or 'Old Teacher'. Historians have speculated as to the real man behind the title. It is, now, generally agreed that the name refers to a Chinese philosopher who was born in Anhui's Woyang county in sixth century BCE. According to some researchers, Lao Tzu did not even refer to a historical person but was most likely an amalgam for many different philosophers who existed before Confucius.

What is known about the life of Lao Tzu comes from a historical work titled *Records of the Historian* written by a chronicler known as Ssu-ma Ch'ien who lived in first century BCE. According to this biographical source, Lao Tzu served as the curator of the Royal Library of Chou. But with the deteriorating social and political standards of the time, he became so disillusioned that he decided to leave the capital city in search of a place where he could live in peace and in his own company. However, as he was going out through the western frontier pass, a gatekeeper, Yin his, stopped Lao and requested him to write a book of his maxims. Lao acceded to the request then and there; the result was a book of eighty one short poems titled *Tao Te Ching*, which he then handed to Hsi and disappeared never to be seen again. Despite the lack of verifiable information, Ch'ien writes in his chronicles that Lao lived to a venerable old age.

The *Tao Te Ching* can be roughly translated into English as *The Book of the Way*. The 'way' denoted an ideal direction for human living, marked by simplicity and awareness of the unique natural force that lives within and pulsates through all creations and aspects of the universe. Known as 'Tao', this universal energy was not only life-giving but unifying and simplifying as well. By the latter, Lao did not encourage ignorance, rather an eschewing of mere intellectualism which led to complexities at best and arrogance at worst. Lao advocated living a simple, virtuous life in harmony with Tao and letting its natural flow guide human thoughts and actions.

Lao's anti-intellectual stance underlined his political philosophy too. He believed that just as in personal life, simplicity and innate virtue should guide public life too; in other words, leaders should live unostentatiously and rule without hunger for wealth and power. Though these ideas would be echoed by Confucius later, the two differed in the importance of knowledge—while Confucius would advocate rigorous education and rituals to guide a leader towards a virtuous living, Lao insisted that arid knowledge only complicated things unnecessarily. If human beings were allowed to function according to the natural universal principle of Tao, they would live in harmony with each other and the world. Though Lao recognized that people acted out of self-interest, he still believed that if external rules and regulations did not interfere, they would eventually be able to resolve their differences in accordance with the natural forces of the universe. On the other hand, as soon as humans were bound by artificial and external laws, they felt the need to rebel and thus took recourse to unethical and immoral actions. Thus, a *central* political tenet of Taoism was that rulers should govern according to the principle of 'wu wei', which means not acting against the natural rules of the universe.

The refusal to resist the natural course of things in Taoism was later mistakenly likened to passivity and weakness. Instead, Lao said that when society was in a state of anarchy, the ideal way to behave was to do one's own duty in as calm and orderly manner as possible. This duty entailed observing and acting according to the wisdom embodied in the natural force of the universe. When people would do their duty on an individual level, the entire community, as a whole, would benefit; thus, according to Lao, the *ideal society* functioned on the basis of natural harmonious forces of the universe rather than governed by man-made laws.

Tao, thus, regarded the structure of laws enacted and enforced by governments as not only unnecessary to a harmonious public life, but also contributing to vice and immorality. According to Lao, the artificial network of rules and regulations actually ended up blocking the natural force in the lives of human beings and that laws and governments only led to further anarchy. This was a strong anti-establishment stance and was later challenged by Confucianism, according to which, strict adherence to law and ritualistic behaviour was necessary for an orderly public life. There are many anecdotes about the two philosophers meeting and engaging in political debates, but no such instances can be verified by actual historical sources. Needless to say, Taoism became more popular among the rural and peasant classes as it advocated a simpler way of living in harmony with the natural universal force. Confucianism, on the other hand, held greater sway in courts and amongst the governing class.

DEATH AND LEGACY

Though Confucius held a government appointment in the state of Lu, he eventually gave it up to escape an increasingly bitter political environment. His teachings and writings attracted several disciples and in later life, Confucius is believed to have travelled widely across Eastern China. Finally, he returned to Lu where he passed away in 479 BCE.

Many of Confucius' political tenets appear to counter modern sensibilities of equality and freedom. The most obvious implication of his fundamental emphasis on virtue—the primary quality of a leader—was that democracy had no place in his ideal state. This was because, Confucianism supported the rule of the wise rather than the rule by many. Not only did he think that a limited few – who were truly virtuous – were eligible to rule, but his view of the state determining the nature of the 'good life' of its citizens – and thereby providing for it – clashed with the modern notion of the separation of state and morality. Today's politics of liberalism is deeply suspicious of any move by a government to define a particular way of life as ethical for its citizens, since history has shown that such precepts are deeply interwoven with structures of power and inequality.

However, scholars have noted deeper currents of new political thinking in Confucius' philosophy. Though he did not believe that a country could be ruled by common citizens, the notion that a leader did not qualify as 'ideal' by his lineage but rather by his virtue was in itself a radical notion at the time. Equally forward-looking was the concept of an ideal leader ruling with compassion and by setting an example of moral behaviour instead of using force and coercion.

Though Confucius' political influence was marginal at the time of his death, in the following centuries, his teachings became the cornerstone of Chinese statecraft. During the Han and Tang dynasties, his theories found their way into the state ideology and enjoyed resurgence from the ninth to eleventh centuries as Neo-Confucianism under the Song dynasty. Today, Confucius' teachings resonate with modern readers because of his ideas like benevolence and compassion which underline all humanist philosophies.

«KNOW MORE»

- Confucius was a great believer in treating common illnesses with natural remedies like using Chinese yam to cure exhaustion, mulberry for inner ear problems and dizziness, and buckbean root for the common cold.
- He was also very particular about the way his meat was served at meals—cooked to the right colour, cut in perfect squares and served with the right sauce.

2

PLATO

The corpus of Western political theory is generally traced back to an Athenian philosopher, academician and theorist who incredibly claimed in his *Second Letter* that 'no writing of his will ever exist'. This Athenian is none other than Plato whose works and teachings have influenced centuries of Western philosophy on politics, ethics, aesthetics, cosmology, epistemology and even language.

EARLY LIFE

Believed to be born in 427 or 428 BCE, Plato grew up in an aristocratic family where his privileges extended from material comforts and social regard to educational opportunities. The latter meant that Plato was among the group of scholars who surrounded the most eminent philosopher of the times, Socrates. Since Socrates never wrote anything down, whatever survives of his theories and teachings exist in Plato's writings, most famously in the *Apology of Socrates*.

Socrates' ill-treatment at the hands of the governing

authorities of the time and his death affected Plato deeply and led to his lifelong suspicion of public life. Plato chose to travel through Greece, Italy, Syracuse and Egypt which in turn contributed to his growing learning, before he returned to Athens.

THE REPUBLIC

Plato's most intensive treatment of politics and governance was in his work titled, *Republic*. In this work, Plato showed Socrates engaging in two discussions—one with each of Plato's brothers. Through these discussions, Justice was explained, on both individual and on abstract levels, as well as arguments put forward as to why it was in every person's interest to be just. The title of the dialogue was drawn from Plato's conception of the ideal state led by rulers who were known as 'Guardians' and were philosophers—in other words, rulers who were knowledgeable about ideas of the Good and Just. The next social category in the *Republic* was made up of auxiliaries and soldiers whose responsibility was to guard the state from enemies and invaders. And finally, at the lowest level of the social hierarchy in the *Republic* came the citizens or workers tasked to produce goods and services in the state.

FORMS AND SHADOWS

Ideas have specific meaning in Plato's theories as they indicate the characteristics that can be used to understand a type of being or an entity. For example, a table, despite having varied designs, materials and uses, is, generally, a structure with more than two legs topped by a flat surface. This makes up the idea or 'Form' of a table that is beyond change, and can be thought to constitute an essential truth which is imitated by a human carpenter and given various manifestations.

In other words, Plato said that though an object could have various designs and uses, its idea remained the same. In contrast, the physical manifestation of that object—which humans could perceive through their senses—was inferior to this idea. Plato further developed this notion as the Parable of the Cave into an elaborate treatise of Reality, Understanding and the ultimate Truth of forms.

The Ideas or Forms of Justice and Good were repeatedly investigated in the *Republic*. Through Socrates, Plato asked if it was enough to treat Justice and Good merely as philosophical abstractions; in fact, he believed that they should be related to practical and material realities like the day-to-day living of people as well as the running of governments.

Plato's *Republic* listed other characteristics of the ideal state known as the 'kallipolis', where the rulers did not have families of their own or owned private property. This was because Plato thought that if the Guardians were allowed to accumulate such assets, they would inevitably become greedy and cruel to other citizens rather than rule ideally to further the citizens' well-being. Plato even had a term for the opposite of the ideal city known as '*timocracy*', where the philosopher-king not only begin to gather personal wealth but also ignored other practices such as music and physical exercise that further wisdom.

In a rare instance of an egalitarian approach, the *Republic* allowed, men and women, both to perform the same tasks. Indeed, his Guardians could include leaders from both genders.

SHIP OF THE STATE

Over the course of the text, Plato pondered on what constituted the most just person as well as the desirable political order and found that it was the one devoted to knowledge and philosophical enquiry. In this way, the *Republic* dismissed democracy as the suitable political system for an ideal state. In a famous metaphor of 'the Ship of the State', Plato described how chaos and disaster would ensue in case sailors who had no idea of navigation were allowed to steer the ship, instead of the true captain, who was seen as a mere stargazer and was never allowed to be at the helm. While the inept and greedy sailors stood for the citizens of the state, the true captain here represented the philosopher, who, qualified with knowledge and virtue, would make an ideal ruler of the state.

FOUR FUNDAMENTAL VIRTUES

Plato founded his ideal Republic on four fundamental virtues—justice, courage, moderation and wisdom. He developed the idea that Justice, whether in an individual or a city, was instated when each being performed its proper task; such a being would not suffer any internal conflict and hence, would have no motivation to act unjustly. Courage was not only physical but, more importantly, civic courage which would make people, especially Guardians, uphold laws and virtues essential for a harmonious public life. Moderation was essential for people, to let them know and remain within the limits of a peaceful civic life while Wisdom included knowledge of both the self and of God, expressed as Reason.

The relationship between the individual and the state could actually be summed up in a running trope of the individual/state. Thus, the individual should be controlled by Reason just as the state should be governed by a wise philosopher-king. Likewise, the auxiliaries in the state stood for emotions in the individual, while the citizens represented desires. Just as true happiness for the individual lay in spiritual liberation attained with the help of a beautiful and well-ordered soul, only the state, ruled by justice and virtue, would be governed perfectly.

LAWS

Plato's concern with politics and governance continued in his other famous works, the *Statesman* and the *Laws,* which offered a more detailed exposition of the ideal form of a government that was also the most practical. In these books, the influence of Solon—an Athenian leader who lived around a century before Plato—was clearly noticeable. In the early sixth century BCE, Athens was racked by civil war, and to restore order, Solon made important constitutional reforms based on the principle of *eunomia* or the restoration of the righteous order. Like Solon, Plato too recognized that among the most crucial challenges faced by the state were those of social diversity and competing interests since these could lead to internal strife—a situation far more dangerous than invasion by external forces. In order to prevent such inner discontent, Plato recommended social cooperation rather than the victory of select classes built on the ruins of others. While in *Republic* it was left to the wisdom of the philosopher-king to bring about social balance and harmony, in *Laws,* it was the state's legal institution that had the right to mediate to ensure social peace. This change shows Plato moving away from his earlier faith in the aristocracy of the Guardians in the *Republic* to realizing the practical advantage of a more varied political system—in the *Laws*—wherein elements of aristocracy, oligarchy and democracy could better address the needs and interests of different classes. In fact, the ideal legal system of a state was one in which political institutions like the Higher Council, the Elected Council and Popular Assembly were made up of the aristocrats, oligarchs and citizens of the state. Hence, each social tier was duly represented. In these ways, Plato's works examined the complex relationship between the philosophy of politics and actual governance, not only exploring what was just and lawful and what was practical and rational.

Among the difficulties that the modern reader has with Plato is his rejection of democracy as the perfect form of government. What Plato objected to was not so much the principle of freedom that underlines the modern understanding of democracy but the possibility of a kind of mob rule where those without wisdom and virtue might acquire power. In

Laws, Plato advocated a form of government in which the element of freedom is mixed with the element of wisdom. For the highest form of political functioning, it was not enough for a person to have an understanding of the world; Plato believed that true political expertise also included knowledge of oneself and of God—true wisdom.

However, Plato's emphasis on knowing God did not lead in the direction of a theocracy based on blind faith and empty rituals. Indeed, in 'Book II' of the *Republic*, Plato criticized Athenians for believing in tales of gods and heroes who were depicted in the poetry of Homer and Hesiod as swayed by caprice and passions. Instead, Plato advocated for true knowledge of the God who was immortal, the source of Ideal Forms and, hence, was the best guide for mankind in both their personal and public lives. Finally, in the *Laws*, Plato put forward the notion that true political order is embodied not in humans but in God.

DEATH AND LEGACY

Plato died in 347 BCE, but it was a testimony to his overarching eminence that his Academy continued to flourish for another three centuries. Of the scholars graduating from the Academy, Aristotle became the most famous as he extended and qualified many of the philosophical concepts of his teacher. Apart from his illustrious student, Plato's influence remained strong over many centuries, peaking in certain periods like the European Renaissance of the sixteenth and seventeenth centuries as well as in the Romantic poetry of the late eighteenth and early nineteenth centuries in England.

> **«KNOW MORE»**
>
> - After returning from his travels to Athens in 380 BCE, Plato founded his Academy—the earliest precursor of the modern university and hence, of academic institutions.
> - Even a great teacher like Plato did not escape ridicule; crowds, ignorant of his philosophy, would, at times, make rude noises after his speeches.

3
ARISTOTLE

Though Aristotle stepped into the world of philosophy as Plato's student, soon, he charted his own path. Today, he is the most recognizable name in ancient Western philosophy, political theory, logic, aesthetics, ethics and science. His views on political institutions and processes are best expressed in *Politics,* which has continued to influence political scientists and statesmen down the ages. Aristotle's other major works are *Poetics, Rhetoric, Ethics, Prior Analytics* as well as treatises on biology, psychology and even meteorology.

EARLY LIFE

Aristotle was born in 384 BCE in Stagira, northern Greece into a family that was both intellectual and well-connected. His father was the court physician of Macedon and later, Aristotle, himself, was invited by King Philip II to tutor his son, Alexander. Once the young prince took over as king and embarked on an ambitious plan of territorial expansion, Aristotle returned to Athens and a life of academics.

MAJOR WORKS

Aristotle was associated with Plato's Academy for around 20twenty years, first as a student and then as a colleague. Eventually, Aristotle went on to establish his own institution called the 'Lyceum', where he learned, taught and wrote most of his major works. *Politics* can be dated roughly around 350 BCE and consists of eight books. Researchers consider the books to be an extension of Aristotle's writings on ethics titled, *Nicomachean Ethics* as well as *Eudemian Ethics,* which deal with what constitutes 'good living' and hence, outlines a moral code of conduct.

POLITICS–PURPOSE OF THE POLIS OR CITY

In *Politics,* this code of conduct is expanded to a person's civic and social context. Thus, the book deals with the role that the political community and political institutions must play to enable citizens to lead a virtuous life. In this sense, *Politics,* as a book is a guide for rulers and statesmen. IT not only drew from Plato's teachings in the *Republic* and *Laws* but also went further to expand Aristotle's own theory of the ideal state.

One of the earliest subjects of discussion in *Politics* was the City or the Polis—not as it is understood today as an urban area which is a part of the entire nation but an independent political unit that controlled surrounding agricultural areas—a meaning, perhaps, better expressed by the term, 'city state'. According to Aristotle, the main purpose of the city was to make it possible for the citizens to lead a life of virtue and happiness which was to be achieved by ensuring the greatest good for the greatest number. In this sense, a political community for Aristotle was not the rule of a set of laws over a group of people but rather a partnership—a political community was made up of citizens who were partners in achieving a common good.

The other purpose of a city was to enable its citizens also to live well—not just by being comfortable and happy–but also by fulfilling one's 'telos' or the purpose of one's life. And this was possible only within a well-ordered political community which would nurture virtue through education as well as through compliance to laws which told its citizens what should and should not be done. Indeed, Aristotle even went on to demonstrate that it was living in a city that made a citizen—here referring only to free people and not slaves—that made their condition truly human.

One of the most significant part of *Politics* dealt with comparing the city and its citizens to an individual and its body parts. Aristotle adapted this Platonic analogy to drive home the importance of the mutual dependence of a city and its people, besides emphasizing that man was a social animal. Just as a body part like an arm or leg would not exist if the body was not alive, so too human beings needed the city to lead a fully human life. However, for human beings to live together, it was necessary to create laws and administer justice through the use of reason and speech. This would not only make social life possible but in the end would enable virtuous living which, rather than accumulation of wealth, territory or ensuring safety, was the true purpose of a city or political community.

CLASSIFICATION OF GOVERNMENTS

Yet another interesting aspect of *Politics* was the classification of systems of government or what Aristotle termed as the constitution. Based on the number and composition of rulers, he broadly identified them into three types, each with a 'fair' and 'unfair' component. Thus, when all the power was concentrated in the hands of one person, it formed a monarchy but only when that power was exercised for the common good. If the ruler wielded that power to serve just his own ends, it became a tyranny. Similarly, when few people of an elite class ruled for the common good, it was known as aristocracy but when the ruling elite lost sight of the welfare of all its citizens, it turned into an oligarchy. Finally, a government made by the citizens was democracy but could degenerate into anarchy when reason was replaced by mob mentality and the appearance of a demagogue.

REAL GOVERNANCE

Apart from serving as a guide for a ruler, *Politics* was also an analysis of the prevailing political systems of the time—their relative successes and failure as well as how short they fell of the ideal. Aristotle's treatise on various governing systems was supported by an analysis of the political institutions, especially those in power in various Greek city-states at the time. He noted wide-ranging differences in wealth, resources and political classes in these city-states and suggested that all of these would determine the kind of government ideal for each of them. Aristotle also advocated the creation of a middle class which would maintain a kind of balance between the extremely rich and poor in the society. Ideally, a city-state should comprise people belonging to the same status, and the best way to accomplish this is to base it on education and virtue.

Yet, another significant aspect of Aristotle's *Politics* dealt with the separation of powers among the three branches of the government—the legislative, which made the laws, the judiciary, which adjudicated at their base, as well as the executive, which enforced the laws. In his ideal city-state, the rulers were drawn from the leisure class. The younger citizens were tasked with the defence of the state while the older citizens were given the responsibility of ruling it. Farmers and labourers were necessary for the material progress of the state but had no rights. At the bottom of the political order was the class of slaves made up of the labourers.

EDUCATION OF THE YOUNGER GENERATION

Politics ended with Aristotle's recommendations on how the younger generation was to be educated. These precepts covered in Book VIII were relevant to the children of the citizens and not for the slaves or other working classes. He believed that education of the young was too important to be left to individual families. He rather advocated that training of such children should be common since the purpose of civic life was for a common good. The ideal curriculum would train both the body and mind. Thus, apart from reading and writing, music, drawing and physical education should also be taught to the citizens of the future. The purpose of this education was neither the acquisition of theoretical knowledge necessary for philosophers nor the practical skills necessary for craftsmen. Instead, it was the product knowledge necessary to fulfil the telos of citizens.

To a great extent, Aristotle's political theories were drawn from his travels as well as experience of diverse governments across and around Greece. Though his teachings in Athens were highly influential, they could not withstand actual political vicissitudes. With the premature death of Emperor Alexander in 323 BCE and consequent fall of the pro-Macedonian government in Athens, Aristotle's position became dangerous and he fled Athens for Chalcis, where he would remain until his death, a year later.

LEGACY

To the modern student, several political precepts by Aristotle seem unfair and discriminatory. His notion of democracy prevented, most conspicuously, women and the labouring class from having any political say. He also advocated the use of slavery and believed that the system offered benefits to both the master and the slave. At the same, it is worth noting that he advised against excessive force and rigidity in the system, and his own will mentioned that his slaves should be set free after his death.

Aristotle's opinion regarding women was even more ambiguous. In keeping with the natural law that granted power to the human over plants and master over the slave, he believed that men too had power over their women. But while slaves did not possess the faculty of 'reason' or 'deliberate quality', women had it but 'lacked authority', according to Aristotle. By extension, women were not to participate in politics but look after their home and family to fulfil their 'telos'.

Despite such theories common to the time, many precepts of Aristotle turned out to be equitable in other ways and even forward-looking. The fundamental principle of polity—that the ideal regime ensured common good for all citizens while a deviant regime sought personal power for the ruler—later influenced theories of a welfare state. Finally, the notion of a government run by the citizens—though the term in his time was more restrictive than it now is—laid the foundation of democracy, which, despite its many faults, is still considered the most conducive to the welfare of all the people in a state.

«KNOW MORE»

- Aristotle and Alexander were very close. Knowing his tutor's interest in science, the young Greek Emperor collected specimens from various lands that he invaded.
- Aristotle had a weakness for pickles and he thought camel meat was the most delectable among all kinds.

4

KAUTILYA

Kautilya, also known as Chanakya, was the most famous political thinker of ancient India and the author of *Arthashastra*. Even today, his work is considered to be a classic treatise on statecraft, diplomacy and politics. Kautilya was a counsellor to Chandragupta Maurya who was the founder of the Maurya dynasty that went on to rule almost the entire Indian subcontinent from the third to first century BCE.

EARLY LIFE

Not much is known about Kautilya's childhood, except that he was born probably in 350 BCE into a Brahmin family—the traditional Hindu priestly class. Hence, he had an access to learning. Also known as Vishnugupt and later Chanakya, he continued his higher studies at Taxila—in present-day Pakistan—which was then home to a flourishing university that welcomed scholastic traditions from around the world. For this reason, it is believed that Kautilya not only studied astrology and medicine but also was well acquainted with the facets of Greek and Persian philosophies.

RISE TO POWER

Despite being widely respected as a brilliant professor of political science and economics at Taxila, Kautilya was not satisfied. He travelled to eastern India where Magadha had emerged as the strongest among many smaller states in the wake of Alexander's departure. Initially, Kautilya tried to seek a position at the court of the Nanda dynasty, which was then ruling Magadha, but he was humiliated and rejected. Thereupon, Kautilya decided to support Chandragupta who was also a Nanda prince but had been exiled from Magadha. Chandragupta managed to raise an army to mount a military challenge to the Nanda ruler. However, it was mainly the civil war in Magadha, resulting from the machinations of the secret intelligence network under Chanakya's directions that deposed the Nanda king. In 322 BCE, Chandragupta finally ascended the throne at Pataliputra, the capital city of Magadha. With his ascension, the Maurya dynasty was founded which continued until 185 BCE. It stretched from southeast Iran in the west to Assam in the east, from the boundaries of the Himalayas in the north to beyond the Deccan in the south.

KAUTILYA'S ARTHASHASTRA

With rising power of the Mauryan empire, Kautilya's prestige as Emperor Chandragupta's chief counsellor also grew. Kautilya eventually put his political philosophy in writing and the result was an expansive treatise titled *Arthashastra*. Though 'Artha', in Sanskrit, literally translates into material resources, the work was actually a compilation of past writings as well as Kautilya's own views on politics, administration, economics and the philosophy behind running a kingdom.

Divided into fifteen sections, each of them has been treated as a separate topic ranging from justice and war to prison administration and coinage. However, the topics dealt with most extensively are diplomacy and war. Kautilya believed that diplomatic relations should be made in such a way by a king that they always benefit his kingdom. The methods to do this covered an elaborate network of treaties and relationships which could, however, be violated to suit the interests of one's own kingdom. At the core of his theories on diplomacy was the Mandala concept based on concentric circles of friends and foes with the central point being the king and his State. Depending on whether the king was facing a superior, inferior or an equal, Chanakya outlined six forms of diplomacy—sandhi, vigraha, asana, dwaidibhava, samsarya and yana—which could be lucidly translated as friendship, hostility, indifference, duality, protection and attack, respectively.

FUNDAMENTAL TENETS

Kautilya's political philosophy was fundamentally motivated by the search for power. He believed that a king could help his kingdom to be perfectly happy only when he possessed absolute power and the way to attain this power was by force or in other words, war. Kautilya advocated three types of war—open or military conflict on the battleground, concealed war similar to guerrilla tactics and the silent war fought with a powerful espionage network to maintain the king's authority.

Kautilya's unsentimental use of force and espionage—even to the extent of killing rebellious family members has been likened to Machiavelli's political philosophy elaborated in *Il Principe*. Apart from the fact that the Italian nobleman was writing around seventeen centuries later and in prison while Kautilya was involved in the day-to-day practicalities of statecraft, the latter has been wrongly interpreted by Western historians as merely a pre-Machiavellian figure. Kautilya actually wrote at length about Justice in his *Arthashastra*, where he strongly advocated a rule of law in criminal and civil justice. For these recommendations of war and spying, Kautilya was exacting in how a ruler should treat defeated kings, generals and soldiers. He also suggested that in internal governance, where force and punishment could be avoided by paying fines and such measures, it should be done likewise. Kautilya, in fact, placed great importance on the protection of wealth and property rights, which formed the rationale to the title of his work. Above all, a just king was one who put the welfare of his citizens as the ultimate goal of his power and success.

Apart from *Arthashastra*, another book attributed to Kautilya is *Chanakya-Neeti*—a collection of aphorisms on statecraft and governance sourced from ancient texts.

DEATH AND LEGACY

It is not clear how Kautilya died but his death is dated around 275 BCE during the reign of Bindusara, the second Mauryan ruler. Kautilya's enormous contributions to statecraft and polity primarily lie in the *Arthashastra* which continued to act as a highly practical guide for many generations of rulers in India. Even though many Western statesmen like Bismarck, Churchill and Woodrow Wilson were probably unacquainted with Kautilya and his work—the pioneer's precepts on diplomacy, war and governance have time and again been reflected in the workings of modern international relations.

«KNOW MORE»

- Kautilya's famed ruthlessness in protecting his king spawned many legends. According to one, he instructed Emperor Chandragupta to consume small doses of poison with his food to make him immune to poisoning attempts by his enemies.
- Kautilya was also called Chanakya after his father's name, Chanak.

5

AL-FARABI

Al-Farabi was a philosopher living in the first century BCE whose thoughts on mankind and society accorded him the status of the founding father of philosophy in the Islamic world. Later generations of Middle Eastern scholars such as Maimonides, Avicenna and Averroes, who, in turn, were widely read by European Renaissance scholars, acknowledged Al-Farabi's influence on their teachings.

EARLY LIFE

Born as Abu Nasr Al-Farabi in 870 CE in present-day Kazakhstan, he spent the major part of his adult life writing and teaching in Baghdad. It is likely that due to the city's worsening political climate, he left the city towards the end of his life and probably spent his remaining days in Damascus, where he died in 950 CE. Not much else is known about the life of the scholar since all the extant sources of biographical information about him date from at least three centuries after his death. Some historians speculate that Al-Farabi may have lived for some time in Byzantium—indicated perhaps by his engagement with Greek language and philosophy—but such a line of thought has not been corroborated by research.

Al-Farabi's mentioned works in later historical texts revealed that not even half of the scholar's writings have been discovered so far. His surviving works, however, gave proof of an intellectual breadth that ranged from music and metaphysics to logic, physics and politics. Additionally, his commentaries on Plato and Aristotle were valuable not only for better understanding of the ancient Greek philosophers but also for gauging the concerns and brilliance of Al-Farabi's own intellect.

MAJOR WORKS

In the manner of the academic disciplines of the time, Al-Farabi's writings on politics and government were interwoven with his ethical and metaphysical views. The two major works of political philosophy attributed to him and brilliantly translated by Muhsin Mahdi and Charles Butterworth are titled, *The Virtuous City* and *The Political Regime*.

The Virtuous City clearly shows the influence of classical Greek philosophers like Plato in its descriptions of the ideal city as well as the characteristics of the perfect ruler. The importance of such themes for Al-Farabi can be gauged from the fact that though he never gave a formal title to

https://thegreatthinkers.org/al-farabi/major-works/book-of-the-opinions-of-the-inhabitants-of-the-virtues-city/
https://plato.stanford.edu/entries/al-farabi/

his philosophy of religion, to discuss his 'philosophy of society', he coined the term *falsafa madaniyya* which dealt with the madina or the civil society. This was similar to the polis as understood in Aristotle's *Politics*, as well as its political hierarchy and administration. Again, the influence of classical Greek scholars in his works is unmistakable. Drawing from the Aristotelian tradition of *Nicomachean Ethics*, Al-Farabi's work on political life contained to a large extent the philosophy of ethical living of the individual. In other words, the *falsafa madaniyya* belonged to the philosophy that explored the concept of the *kamal al-insan*, the perfection of man as an individual.

In line with its classical predecessor, Al-Farabi's *The Virtuous City* thus defined the ideal regime where people come together to cooperate, perform noble activities and lead a life of virtue and happiness. According to Al-Farabi, the faculty of rational thinking differentiated man from divine beings as well as animals. Therefore, his attainment of civic well-being depended upon the knowledge of the difference between the noble and the base, vice and virtue and using that discrimination to perform virtuous deeds.

A significant part of *The Virtuous City* dealt with the classification of social classes, generic descriptions of various types of governments and its leaders. According to Al-Farabi, his ideal society could be divided into three classes of people, some more than others, depending upon their rank in the citizenry (class). These three classes were: the wise or 'philosophers' who, with the help of their highly developed intellectual faculties, understood the true nature of things;

the followers of these philosophers who trusted the latter's insights and, therefore, learnt about the nature of things from the philosophers and finally; the ordinary citizens forming the majority who could know about the nature of things only through similitude.

Al-Farabi also devoted a section in his book on the characteristics of the Ideal ruler of the Virtuous city. Apart from making laws, leading in war and providing education, the main job of the ruler was to order the social classes in the hierarchy of their natural virtue so that each was given an opportunity to develop their capabilities and serve the superior class. Such an arrangement of the socio-political hierarchy in such a city would then reflect the celestial pattern of the cosmos, which, because of its harmonious functioning, stood for perfection.

CLASSIFICATION OF ACTUAL REGIMES

The Political Regime also began with the cosmological hierarchy standing for the perfect system that an ideal city should imitate in its own political arrangement. Eventually, however, the book departed from *The Virtuous City* and emphasized on describing the workings of the actual political systems of the world. Al-Farabi identified three such regimes, delineating each by the degree of their difference from the guiding principle of the Ideal regime. The first was the practice of true knowledge and virtue, which led to the activities conducive to true happiness. In contrast, he described the first as 'ignorant' regimes, whose citizens did not possess any knowledge about the nature of the world, and hence, engaged in activities devoid of virtue. Such people pursued baser goals, good or bad, in complete ignorance of what constituted true happiness. The second was the immoral regime made up of people who were aware of what virtuous actions were and yet they were busy in accumulating wealth, territory, power and so on. The third, Al-Farabi categorized as the 'erring' regimes whose citizens had come to acquire mistaken or corrupt notions of the meaning of virtue and purported goal of their lives. Such a regime was probably founded on erroneous and corrupt ideals at the very outset or ideal principles but then was corrupted over time with the indoctrination of false or wicked ideas and principles.

OTHER WORKS

In all these ways, Al-Farabi revealed that his precepts about the ideal city were not restricted to the world of abstractions. Instead, he evaluated the *madina* and its ruling elite on the basis of its success in guiding the citizens towards a life of individual virtue. In a leader who ruled by his intelligence and wisdom, he combined the qualities of the philosopher and the prophet. This was important to Al-Farabi because a coming together of the divine and politics indicated the political importance of holding the right beliefs about God, the world and man.

It was also in this context that Farabi developed his philosophy of religion. In fact, he saw religion as the instrument which could most effectively guide both individuals as well as societies towards virtuous existence. In this way, Al-Farabi's notion of religion did not claim to be the fountainhead of wisdom and truth in isolation but rather functioned as a discipline meant to be applied to achieve human and social perfection.

Other books by Al-Farabi such as *Selected Aphorisms* and *The Enumeration of Sciences* reveal a close comparison of political philosophy with other branches of study. According to him, it was necessary for administrators to get an education in theoretical sciences so that they would be able to ensure: firstly, that every citizen learned the skills necessary to achieve individual felicity; secondly, that each citizen performed functions in keeping with his place in society. In this way, individual felicity or happiness was woven with the cosmological model of a well-ordered society. Not surprisingly then, the book of Religion concludes with the proposal of the ideal city being governed by a collaboration between the devout Islamic scholar and a secular philosopher so that it would embody both qualities of knowledge and virtue.

LEGACY

The themes and style of many of Al-Farabi's writings, as well as his own commentaries on Plato and Aristotle, indicate the influence of Greek philosophy and sciences on the Islamic scholar. The parallels drawn between the cosmological order and its political hierarchy of the ideal city are among the most definitive indication of such influences. Though his source was classical Greek thought, he was always conscious of writing for an Islamic populace, which is indicated by his pre-occupation with the reality of wars, laws of succession, jurisprudence and, especially, the afterlife as well as the notion that political practice should operate within the framework of many Ummahs or nations.

> «KNOW MORE»
>
> - Apart from the political, religious and ethical philosophy, Al-Farabi also wrote a book on music titled *Kitab al-Musiqa*, as well as a treatise elaborating on the therapeutic effects of music on the human soul.
> - The main-belt asteroid 7057 Al-Farabi was named in the honour of this most famous of medieval Islamic philosophers.*

---

*https://en.wikipedia.org/wiki/Al-Farabi#cite_note-MPC-Al-F%C4%81r%C4%81b%C4%AB-84. Last accessed on 07 January 2019.

6

MAIMONIDES

Maimonides was the most famous philosopher in medieval Judaism and is best known today for codifying Jewish law in Hebrew as well as Arabic. Besides law and governance, religion and medicine were other subjects on which Maimonides wrote extensively which came to influence subsequent philosophers in Judaism.

EARLY LIFE

Born as Moses Ben Maimon on 30 March 1135 CE in Cordoba, Spain, the philosopher went by the Arabic name of Abu Imran Musa ibn Maymun ibn Ubayd Allah or simply, Rambam. Maimonides grew up in a learned Jewish family and received instruction in different sciences from various tutors, including his father.

However, young Moses soon found his family in a difficult situation as the Almohad sect of Islam conquered Cordoba and this forced Jews living there to either adopt Islam or leave the city. For eleven years, Moses and his family struggled to accommodate to the political exigencies—outwardly adopting Islamic practices but continuing with the Jewish ways in the privacy of their home. Eventually, the stress of living a dual existence proved too disturbing and they moved to Fez in Morocco in 1159 AD, hoping to live anonymously. Here, Moses picked up his studies in Greek philosophy and Rabbinic literature that had been suspended due to political vicissitudes and added medicine to his studies as well. But when a friend of Moses was executed for being a practicing Jew, the family moved again. Their new destination was Palestine which, though marginally safer, offered little means of livelihood. Once more, the family relocated themselves, this time in Egypt where Jews were legally allowed to practice their faith but barred by law from lapsing into Judaism once converted to Islam. Indeed, Moses himself was arrested once on suspicion of being a renegade Muslim but was released after being able to prove that he had never converted to Islam in the first place.

The long experience of living on the edge of what is and is not legal because of his faith naturally turned Maimonides towards examining the laws of Judaism in all their complexities. His first major work was *Kitab al-Siraj*, a commentary on the *Mishna* or the collection of oral laws in Judaism. Maimonides's work helped to clarify several concepts, which had become obscure due to their oral transmission. However, Maimonides's most significant work was *Mishne Torah* or *The Torah Reviewed*, which was the codification of Jewish law. The project took ten years to complete and eventually, turned out to be one of the foundation texts of the Jewish faith. The other major work was *A Guide for the Perplexed*. It advocated a life guided by reason and moderation rather than dogma and extremism.

POLITICAL PHILOSOPHY

Though Maimonides did not write any exclusive political text, his major works revealed an abiding concern with the relationship between human conduct and the law of the society. The most famous essay in the commentary on *Mishna* found in the introduction to *Pereq Ḥeleq* or *Tractate Sanhedrin*, chapter ten for example included 'Thirteen Principles of Faith', which he believed were necessary to follow in the ideal state of Jews. Again, in his introduction to *Tractate Aboth*, Maimonides described what constituted a virtuous human action which, in turn, drew from the Aristotelian tradition of *Nicomachean Ethics*.

The mark of classical Greek political philosophy was even more distinct in *Mishne Torah* which began with the Aristotelian idea of mirroring of cosmological order in the ideal civic society. The major trait of such a state was that there is no conflict between the laws and philosophy. In fact, the perfect execution of Laws would require an appreciation of philosophical concepts of the human being and the world. In keeping with this view, Maimonides imagined the Messianic period as one which would perfectly mirror the order of the natural world and in which its citizens would live by the Law. Indeed, such an arrangement would be most conducive to political peace and harmony which, in turn, would help Israel to achieve the highest spiritual actualization.

GUIDE TO THE PERPLEXED

The complex relationship between Law and philosophy became one of the main themes of *The Guide to the Perplexed*. Originally written in Judeo-Arabic as *Dalalat al-ḥairin*, the book was first translated into Hebrew in 1204 by a contemporary of Maimonides, Samuel ben Judah ibn Tibbon, under the title, *Moreh Nevukhim*. Maimonides wrote the *Guide* as a series of letters to a former student named Jacob ben Judah of Ceuta. It was in response to the student's difficulty in reconciling his understanding of Reason and Science with his faith in Judaism as a revealed religion. According to Maimonides, such apparent contradictions were due to a faulty understanding of either the *Bible* or the ancient philosophers. For him, there was no conflict between Reason and Faith because both originated in God. While most of the *Guide* addressed philosophical questions and how they could be answered by Religion, 'Part Three' of the book dealt specifically with human actions. This again revealed the influence of Aristotle's *Ethics*, especially as it related to Maimonides's vision of the Ideal City. The perfect citizen of such a city was described as having traits of both the philosopher and statesman so that his actions would lead both to personal improvement, as well as the benefit of the society as a whole.

Interestingly, Maimonides clarified in the Introduction to the *Guide* that it should be read by someone who possessed thorough grounding scientific disciplines and philosophical inquiry. Otherwise, it would do more harm than good to the uninformed reader. Mindful of the possibility of his *Guide* being misinterpreted as the rejection of all Laws in society, he wrote in the Introduction that at times, he had to take recourse to literary subterfuge and deliberate ambiguity to mask his true meaning from the undiscerning readers. Indeed, as feared by Maimonides, *The Guide for the Perplexed* did go on to rouse the anger of a section of contemporary Jewish Rabbis who objected to his rationalist views regarding angels, prophecy and miracles. They particularly objected to Maimonides's claim that the biblical account of the Creation could have been reconciled to the Aristotelian doctrine of the eternity of the universe if the ancient Greek had presented proofs that are more conclusive. In later centuries too, the *Guide* came to be considered heretical in certain sections of Judaism, though in the modern world, its significance as a work of both religion and philosophy has been established.

OTHER WORKS

Apart from these major works, Maimonides wrote several legal treatises like those on logic as well as letters on subjects ranging from religion to astrology. Of particular note are his eleven short volumes on medicine which were widely respected not only for their careful observation but also for their simplicity of expression and ease of access.

Maimonides, after a life of wandering, finally found success and acceptance in Egypt as a medical practitioner, even becoming the court physician to the famous Muslim military leader, the Sultan Saladin, and his son al-Afḍal. The high professional regard he commanded is evident from the fact that he had a busy private practice, and was even invited by state hospitals to deliver lectures on complex medical topics before his fellow physicians. After achieving some degree of personal and professional stability, he got married and had a son named Abraham who grew up to be a Jewish scholar. By the time of Maimonides's death on 13 December 1204, he was a revered member of the Jewish community in Egypt, guiding them in times of social and personal difficulties.

LEGACY

Maimonides's codification of the religious and civic laws of Judaism is regarded as a milestone in Judaic scholarship. Judaism, like Christianity and Islam, is a revealed religion, meaning a religion based on divine revelation, usually through prophets. Though Maimonides's rational stance on Judaism as a revealed religion was met with some opposition in his time, eventually his works came to be regarded among the foundations of Jewish faith. His medical works, too, are honoured with a significant place in the history of medical science. Indeed, Maimonides's influence extended beyond medieval Judaic philosophy and over time, influenced Christian theorists such as Thomas Aquinas and Duns Scotus, as well as later thinkers like Benedict de Spinoza and G.W. Leibniz, especially in the context of the relation between philosophy and theism.

«KNOW MORE»

- Maimonides's 'Thirteen Principles of Faith' continues to be recited in present-day synagogues across the world.
- Many popular quotes are attributed to Maimonides:
  - Truth does not become more true by virtue of the fact that the entire world agrees with it, nor less so even if the world disagrees with it.
  - No disease that can be treated by diet should be treated by other means.

7

THIRUVALLUVAR

Thiruvalluvar was a celebrated philosopher and poet from Tamil Nadu in southern India. He wrote *Thirukkurral*—a treatise on matters ranging from ethics and governance to economics and love. Thiruvalluvar's works went on to greatly influence Tamil literature and the whole of Dravidian culture.

EARLY LIFE

Historians have not been able to find incontrovertible evidence of Thiruvalluvar's date and place of birth. He is said to have lived sometime between fourth century BCE and seventh century CE. While his Tamil origins are beyond doubt proved, there is disagreement regarding his place of birth. According to some, he was born in Madurai while others believe it was Mayilapuram or modern-day Mylapore in Chennai. In 2005, a 3-member research team from the Kanyakumari Historical and Cultural Research Centre determined that Thirunayanarkurichi, a village in present-day Kanyakumari district, was the birthplace of Thiruvalluvar.

Again, in keeping with the controversial biographical details of Thiruvalluvar, his religious affiliation is also a subject of speculation and scholars have variously claimed him to be a Jain, Hindu or Buddhist saint-poet.

MAJOR WORK

Thiruvalluvar is best known today as the author of *Thirukkurral*, a great literary work, written in the form of couplets which deal with varied subjects like ethics, politics and love. However, dating the work has been a problem. Traditionally, *Thirukkurral* was hailed as the final and finest literary flowering of the third Sangam literature—a period of Tamil secular literary outpouring in ancient southern India roughly between 300 BCE to 300 CE. Among scholars who ascribed to this view, some like Somasundara Bharathiar and M. Rajamanickam dated *Thirukkurral* as early as 300 BCE while others like K.K. Pillay believed it might have been written in early first century CE.

However, some scholars believe that *Thirukkurral* was not part of Sangam literature at all, and was written much later. Most notable among them was Czech linguist Kamil Zvelebil who assigned it to a period between 450 and 500 CE. Based on the presence of Sanskrit loanwords as well as later grammatical innovations, Zvelebil believed *Thirulkurral* could not have existed in the time of Sangam literature. Despite its uncertain origins, *Thirukkurral* eventually became famous as a treasure house of ethics and philosophy across the world. This much-deserved success was made possible to a great extent by the late-seventeenth-century Latin translation of the text by Italian Jesuit priest Constanzo Beschi, thus introducing the text to the rest of the world.

Thirukkurral is composed into 133 sections, each having 10 couplets or *kurrals*. Sections 1 to 38 make up the Book of Virtue or Dharma, which, in Tamil, loosely translates as *Aram*. Thus, the *Book of Aram* explains virtues that do not depend on surroundings, like righteousness, veracity, non-violence and lifestyle matters like vegetarianism.

BOOK OF PORUL

The next part of *Thirukkurral* and its longest is known as the *Book of Porul,* which moves from the inner life of virtue to the public life of the citizen. *Porul* roughly translates into wealth or polity and contains the core of Thiruvalluvar's ideas on political governance, ethics, law as well as material assets. This book is made up of seventy chapters, each containing ten couplets, making a total of 700 couplets which describe how a person should deal with public matters—in other words, virtues that depend on the surroundings.

Porul is explained on both public and private levels; in the former, the couplets describe the social, legal and economic rights and obligations of the government and how to run the administration in an ideal state. On the individual level, the couplets lay out ways to achieve, maintain and protect one's wealth and property, how to make a living and be assured of financial security. Economic prosperity and good governance at private and public levels respectively are understood as important pursuits in the life of human beings, which the *Book of Porul* helps its readers to achieve.

The last part of the *Thirukkurral* is the *Book of Inbam* or *Inbattuppal*, which refers to the pursuit of conjugal love. Composed of twenty-five chapters, the book includes 250 couplets, which talk about the duties of an individual with regard to a conjugal relationship.

While the *Thirukkurral* deals with the ethical, public and love lives of people, it is far from a long dry treatise. The impact of this literary work comes with its poetic force. Written in aphoristic couplets, the books can be read as parts of a complex structure with one virtue acting as the foundation stone for the next or just for the pleasure of their pithy sayings.

LEGACY

Like other biographical details, the year and place of Thiruvalluvar's death are not known. However, his ideas in *Thirukkurral* have had enormous influence on Indian, especially Dravidian, political, religious and social philosophy. Many of his couplets opposed the ingrained traditions of the time. One such especially radical idea was his dismissal of the caste system. He explicitly said in one couplet that, 'One is not great because of one's birth in a noble family; one is not low because of one's low birth.' Additionally, he pointed out that people should perform good deeds for the sake of leading a virtuous life and not with thoughts of rewards in the afterlife. Far more concrete was his influence in matters of agriculture and administration. For example, inspired by Thiruvalluvar's ideas on how to improve the economic condition of the people, the Chola king, Karikala, of the first century CE ordered large-scale agrarian reforms as well as development measures such as land reclamation and dam construction projects.

Thiruvalluvar's precepts on statecraft in the *Thirukkurral* have often given way to comparisons between him and other thinkers of ancient India who codified social and public laws. But while the *Manusmriti* strongly advocates the caste system with all its inequalities, the *Thirukkurral* puts forward a more humane social structure. Again, while Kautilya's *Arthashastra* firmly believes in the use of force, espionage and even duplicity in maintaining the sovereign's authority, Thiruvalluvar's precepts are firmly grounded in morality and benevolence; for example, the latter speaks in favour of taxation by consent, whereas the *Arthashastra* had suggested means like punishment, if necessary, to raise government revenues. In all these ways, Thiruvalluvar's ideas on polity and statecraft were innovative for his times and anticipated the ideals of humanity and equality of today.

«KNOW MORE»

- In 1968, the Tamil Nadu government made it compulsory for every government bus to display a Kural couplet.
- A 133-feet statue of Thiruvalluvar stands tall at one of the islands near Kanyakumari on the southernmost tip of the Indian peninsula.

8

NICCOLÒ MACHIAVELLI

Machiavelli was a diplomat, statesman and administrator of the Italian Renaissance. He was the first to separate political virtues from morality and religion which eventually became one of the most definitive traits of modern political systems. His best-known work today is *The Prince* or *Il Principe* in which he portrays, with a steely realism, the qualities that a successful ruler must possess. Though Machiavelli's views have been criticized for their pessimistic and unethical orientation, they eventually came to be influential for their pragmatic and objective value.

EARLY LIFE

Niccolò Machiavelli was born on 3 May 1469 in Florence, Italy. Though the family had a long history of service in the Florentine government, his father, Bernado, was barred from holding public office due to financial irregularities and was forced to earn a living from a small property located outside the city. Young Niccollò, however, managed to get a well-rounded education during the height of the Italian Renaissance. Aided with a resourceful and enterprising nature, Machiavelli managed not only to get a government appointment at the second chancery or the public archives of the Florentine Republic but quickly became its top official as well. At the age of 29, he was already heading the republic's foreign affairs in subject territories.

Over a fourteen-year career at the chancery, Machiavelli was in charge of as many as forty diplomatic missions, among which the most important ones were to the court of France, Cesare Borgia, Pope Julius II, the court of Holy Roman Emperor Maximilian I and Pisa. During this time, he saw the rise and fall of many powerful rulers like Borgia which led him to write short tracts such as *On the Way to Deal with the Rebel Subjects of the Valdichiana* and poems like *First Decennale*.

IMPRISONMENT AND EXILE

The wheel of fortune and power, in time, began to go down for Machiavelli as well. In 1512, the Republic of Florence was deposed and the de Medici family came back to rule. Machiavelli was accused of conspiracy and treason which led to his torture, imprisonment and, finally, exile to his father's old property in San Casciano.

Like the pragmatist he was, Machiavelli used the years of exile to read and write. His reading consisted of histories of ancient Roman empires and republics. In around 1513, he began writing his own theories on what he considered essential traits of a leader for him to be successful. The result was *The Prince* or *Il Principe* in Italian, which would get published only in 1532, five years after his death, though there is evidence that it was in private circulation during Machiavelli's lifetime under a Latin title, *De Principatibus* or *Of Principalities*. The book began with Machiavelli's dedication to Lorenzo de' Medici and ended with the fervent hope of Italy's political resurgence and military success. In keeping with the spirit of Renaissance, Machiavelli rejected Latin—the classical language for scholarly work—to write the book in native Italian.

IL PRINCIPE

For the first time in the history of political philosophy, there was a book not concerned with how the ruler should ideally behave or the state should ideally function but rather what would and would not make him successful. The separation of the field of ethics and governance—that were entwined in the philosophies of ancient Greeks—was a novel way of looking at civic life. The guiding principle in this field was that 'of necessity', according to which the ruler—most often addressed as a New Prince—might use or discard both personal morals as well as principles of governance. Machiavelli also adopted the same matter-of-fact attitude to history, which he saw merely as a series of physical events, with no teleology or any baggage of transcendent meaning.

Significantly, Machiavelli was the first in the history of Western Philosophy to recognize politics as a form of power play. In the book, he laid out an understanding of politics as the struggle to acquire, maintain and consolidate political power. Machiavelli agreed with ancient philosophers like Plato that rulers are not subject to the same virtues as the private citizens. However, Machiavelli went on to show that 'virtu' in his writings acquires newer shades of meaning. Thus, princely virtue went beyond moral goodness—it meant being self-reliant and well versed with the art of war, seeking not just security but also glory which, in turn, increased the chances of being a stronger ruler.

Contrary to popular opinion, Machiavelli never wrote, 'the end justifies the means'. Instead, he came up with a far less catchy maxim, 'One must consider the final result,' which meant that for a ruler, the ultimate goal should always be the preservation of the state and to this end, he could use any means, without regard to any moral rules. Indeed, he went on to illustrate his precepts with the mention of real-life rulers and their political actions, evaluating them according to their final performance—whether or not they eventually achieved the goals that they had set for themselves in the beginning. Based on such observations, he then gave practical suggestions to the Prince, notwithstanding their moral implications.

OTHER WORKS

The other book that Machiavelli was writing around this time was *The Discourse on Livy*, wherein he compared the ancient Roman forms of government to present-day corruption and weakness of Italian states. Though the *Discourse* contained many passages on the value of a republican form of government, ultimately, Machiavelli appeared to favour the belief that the state was stronger when run by a single leader. Machiavelli's comparison of the Ancients and Moderns generally had a central political point, which showed how the tradition of Christianity and its moralizing weakened rulers and political systems. And yet, it would be a mistake to regard Machiavelli as merely the champion of absolutism. *The Discourse on Livy* contains many passages where he praises a republic for its civic virtues, patriotism and free political participation.

In 1520, with the death of the reigning Medici scion, an opportunity opened up for Machiavelli to regain political goodwill. He was commissioned by Pope Leo X to write a history of Florence from its origin to the death of Lorenzo di Piero de' Medici in 1492, which after a series of stops and starts, took the form of *Florentine Histories*. In this book, Machiavelli went back to his favourite comparison of the weaknesses of Florence to the strength of classical Roman rulers but he realized that he had to tread a fine line between his critiques and giving offence to his Medici patrons.

Machiavelli evidently managed his prospects with delicacy for soon after. In April 1526, he was given a government appointment of the chancellor of the Procuratori delle Mura to supervise Florence's fortifications. However, with the downfall of the Medicis, the newly formed Republican government refused to reinstate Machiavelli back to his former position in the Chancery—a denial which Machiavelli took quite hard as within a month he fell ill and died on 21 June 1527.

LEGACY

Machiavelli's influence can be clearly mapped on later philosophers. His understanding of civic life as the struggle for power was echoed in successive political thinkers, from Thomas Hobbes and Harrington in the seventeenth century, James Madison and Alexander Hamilton in the following century to Robert Michels and Pareto Mosca in the nineteenth century, and more recently, in the writings of Robert A. Dahl, Morton Kaplan and Hans Morgenthau. Echoes of Machiavelli's amoral politics can be found in German thinkers like the historian, Friedrich Meinecke and the philosopher, Ernst Cassirer who too rejected the ethical underpinnings of politics and statecraft.

Additionally, Machiavelli was one of the earliest to advocate coming together of different Italian principalities. For this reason, his works would go on to become a significant force during the nineteenth century Italian Risorgimento or the Italian unification.

Most significantly, Machiavelli was the first political philosopher to break away from the tradition of the ideal city-state as delineated in Plato's *Republic* and Saint Augustine's *City of God* to show the actual working of the state and its ruler. In this sense, his book *The Prince* can be regarded as laying the foundation of modern political science—a discipline which is not concerned how the state can be an instrument to serve the cause of justice and morality but how the state's working is an end in itself.

«KNOW MORE»

- The adjective 'Machiavellian' meaning 'devious' comes from Niccolò Machiavelli and is an oversimplification of his political philosophy that advocated separation of morality and statecraft.
- Nazi leader Adolf Hitler was supposed to have kept a copy of *The Prince* by his bedside, while Italian dictator Mussolini wrote a foreword to an edition of the book.
- Machiavelli's *Il Principe* was a topic of avid discussion in Renaissance England and Shakespeare used his name on at least three occasions in his plays, one of them being, like 'murderous Machiavel' in *Henry VI, Part III*. However, according to critics, the character of Richard III in the eponymously titled play comes closest to the popular model of the political schemer who would do anything to realize his political ambitions.

9

THOMAS HOBBES

Thomas Hobbes was a seventeenth-century English philosopher whose social contract theory went on to serve as the founding stone of Western political philosophy for many centuries to come. Though his theory is put forward most elaborately in *Leviathan*, other works which expounded his political philosophy were *Elements of Law* and *De Cive* or *On the Citizen*.

EARLY LIFE

Born on 5 April 1588 in the English town of Westport, Hobbes had a chequered childhood. even though a vicar, his father fell afoul of the law and disappeared, leaving behind a family of three children who were then brought up by young Hobbes's uncle. However, the boy's natural inclination towards academics meant that when he was just fourteen, Hobbes was able to secure a place in Magdalen Hall, Oxford, for further studies. In 1608, he left Oxford upon an invitation by Lord Cavendish of Hardwick (who would later become the first Earl of Devonshire) to tutor his eldest son, William Cavendish. In this appointment, Hobbes was able to travel widely through Europe and benefit from interaction with other writers and thinkers like Ben Jonson and Francis Bacon. More importantly, being part of the Cavendish household exposed him to regular discussions on political matters like governance, duties and rights of the king, the parliament and so on.

POLITICAL FERMENT

The decades of the twenties and thirties in seventeenth-century England were a time of continuing political ferment. The optimism in the wake of James I's ascension to the throne in 1603 and the unification of England and Scotland had waned. Increasingly, the king and the parliament came into conflict over the scope of royal powers, especially in the matter of raising money for defence-related expenses. This, in turn, was interwoven with disputes between the Puritans, who opposed Roman Catholic influence in religious and political institutions, and Conformists, who viewed the Puritan demands as seditious actions against the king. All these strands of conflict came to head in 1642 when Charles I was executed and England became a Republic under the leadership of Oliver Cromwell.

Not surprisingly, Hobbes's political writings during this time reflect his concerns at hand. What is equally interesting is how he addressed different readers in his different works. In 1640, he wrote the *Elements of Law—Natural and Politick* to help the Royalists understand the challenge to Charles I and the ways of dealing with it.

STATE OF NATURE

With England being declared a Republic, Hobbes fled to France where he lived from 1649 to 1651. In political exile, Hobbes wrote his next work, *De Cive* or *On the Citizen*. Since this treatise was directed at continental scholars, he used Latin, which was still used as the language for academic research. Even though he was using a classical language, Hobbes views were anything but classical. He famously broke with the Aristotelian tradition of *Politics* which proposed that human beings were naturally suited to the life of the 'polis' and could fully realize their potential by leading the life of virtuous citizens. In fact, he went so far as to suggest that instead of serving practical goals, the study of Aristotle's works merely helped in the justification of ambitions of young rebels.

In contrast, Hobbes asserted that human beings were instinctively self-centred, irrational and devoid of self-restraint. Thus, 'the natural condition of mankind' was marked by anarchy and violence in which, each person, however weak and alone, was capable of killing another. Despite such tendencies towards violence, the majority found it impossible to completely defeat competitors to fulfil their own self-interest. Each person lived in fear and distrust, wanting, above all, to preserve their lives and goods; at the same time, most afraid of violence at the hands of others. This desire of mankind to preserve itself in the face of threat or violent death formed the foundation of Hobbesian psychology.

The first step out of such a state of fear and paralysis would have been the collective desire for peace and safety. In such a situation, mankind found it practical to submit to a sovereign and to transfer to him power and their freedom in return for safety and political order. This formed the basis of the social contract. In this sense, the Hobbesian political order was a consciously constructed system designed to remove mankind from a pre-political state of nature to civilized living.

An interesting trait of life in this 'state of nature' was the absence of any natural source of authority which would have enabled humans to order their lives. Thus, despite his arguments in favour of mankind subjecting itself to the rule of a sovereign, Hobbes actually put forward quite a radical idea—saying that no one, not even a monarch had a natural or God-given right to rule over others. This claim, that the monarch ruled not by divine right but popular consent, would go on to anger the Royalists in England.

Though Hobbes recognized that in submitting to a sovereign, the people were giving up their freedom, yet the alternative was the far more frightening prospect of the 'war of every man against every man'. This was a situation of violence and chaos that no citizen would wish for. Hobbes thought that such a 'state of nature' might have occurred at the 'beginning of time' or in primitive societies such as those of the Native Americans. However, at the same time, he wanted to warn his countrymen that they must continue to undermine their king's authority as similar anarchical conditions could well descend upon seventeenth-century England too.

MAJOR WORKS

In the sections on 'Liberty', 'Empire' and 'Religion', *De Cive* goes on to talk exhaustively about these concepts and how a man's best chances of survival and success lay in following his king as the sovereign political power. *De Cive* was actually conceptualized as part of a larger scholarly work titled *Elements of Philosophy* that included two other books, *De Corpore* or *Concerning the Body* and *De Homine* or *Concerning Man*. Among the most interesting parts in this trilogy is Hobbes's own research in optics as well as his evaluation of Galileo's writings on the motions of terrestrial bodies and Keplar's on astronomy.

LEVIATHAN

Nine years after *De Cive*, Hobbes published his magnum opus, *Leviathan* or *The Matter, Form and Power of a Commonwealth, Ecclesiastical and Civil* in which he described in greater detail the need for humans to rise above their 'state of nature' marked by chaos, unchecked self-interest and absence of self-restraint. This could lead to 'the war of all against all' and to prevent it, people had to be brought under the rule of a powerful central authority—imagined here as the Leviathan or a Biblical sea creature. Such power was required not only to keep the ordinary people in awe; a visible reminder of the need to keep the social contract but also as a check on the ambitions of some who desired honour or power more than others.

In *Leviathan,* Hobbes also talked about 'laws of nature' or the steps taken by mankind to move away from the state of nature and sets down nineteen such rules to be followed in society. As in *De Cive,* here too, Hobbes demonstrated how the social contract was not only the sole practical solution to the chaos of social living but also the only moral path for humanity. Hence, *Leviathan* expanded the civil duties of a true Christian by arguing that complete obedience to the sovereign's decrees did not put believers at risk of loss of salvation; instead, it helped them to achieve their spiritual goals better.

The other major concern of *Leviathan* was the influence of Church, especially, the Roman Catholic in civil matters. Hobbes was against the separation of powers not only between Church and State but among the branches of government as well. He firmly believed that all institutions should be under the definitive control of the sovereign authority or else conditions could lead to civil war, the causes of which were dealt with in *Behemoth; or, The Long Parliament* (1679). His descriptions of the fallacies of democracy and the anarchy it could lead to was also one of the underlying concerns of his later writings like his translation—the first in the English language—of Thucydides' *History of the Peloponnesian War.* At the end of his life, he returned to his first love, the classics, and translated Homer's *Iliad* and *Odyssey.*

DEATH AND LEGACY

Hobbes died on 4 December 1679, but not before he had established himself among the strongest, if not popular, thinkers of his age. Many of his concepts like the social contract and the notion that acts are allowed if not clearly forbidden went on to influence later thinkers like John Locke, Rousseau and Kant, besides constituting the building blocks of Western political philosophy for generations to come.

«KNOW MORE»

- His year of birth, 1588, when the English coast was threatened by the Spanish Armada, Hobbes claimed in half-jest that the looming danger of attack brought about his birth–'Mother dear/ Did bring forth twins at once, both me and fear'.
- Hobbes owned a small share in the trading company called 'Virginia Company', that was founded by King James I for the colonization of parts of the eastern coast of North America.

10

JOHN LOCKE

Like Hobbes, John Locke was a seventeenth-century thinker who found in the political tumult of the times, the motivation to frame a political philosophy of his own. However, unlike the former, Locke would interpret the social contract theory in more humanistic terms that would eventually serve as the foundation stone for modern liberalism and democracy.

EARLY LIFE

Born on 29 August 1632, in the village of Wrington in Somerset County, Locke grew up in a well-to-do family. Both his parents were Puritans and loyal to the Republican government that came in power in 1642. Locke was a brilliant student since childhood and while studying at Westminster School in London, earned the distinction of being chosen as a 'King's Scholar'. This gave him the opportunity to study at Christ College at Oxford, where he took up logic, metaphysics and the classical languages. After completing his Masters, Locke was invited to be a tutor at the same college. However, the keen academician that he was, Locke was hungry for more knowledge, and in 1674, he graduated with a degree in medicine as well.

During the course of his medical education, Locke came across Lord Ashley who would later become the Earl of Shaftesbury. Persuaded by the latter to settle in London, Locke not only became the nobleman's personal physician but also began looking after his employer's political and business interests as well.

POLITICAL PHILOSOPHY

Locke's exposure to the heart of English politics in London encouraged him to put his thoughts on paper and the result was his landmark *Two Treatises of Government* which put forward extremely powerful and original ideas concerning the rights of the citizen and the nature of human society. Locke claimed that all humans had certain rights granted to them by God, their Creator and these were the inalienable rights of life, liberty, property and the pursuit of their own goals. As such, their denial by other people or governments was equal to affront to God. He also termed them 'negative rights' as opposed to 'positive rights' such as the right to equality, employment, education and healthcare that would be developed by later political theorists.

Unlike Hobbes who described the 'state of nature' as anarchic and depraved, Locke claimed that life in the natural condition was marked by 'a state of perfect freedom' as well as equality and plenty among men—what it lacked was just 'a common...authority to judge between them'. However, because one of the basic human rights in this state was the right to self-preservation, it made people selfish and also led them to come into conflict with another. This was in keeping with the Hobbesian belief that mankind was driven by self-interest.

LOCKE'S SOCIAL CONTRACT THEORY

Like Hobbes again, Locke too saw the way out of this state of conflict through a social contract. But while the Hobbesian social contract emerged out of human irrationality, greed and inability to defend their own rights, Locke's notion of the social contract was underlined by the principles of individual liberty and equality. Locke believed that it was to protect individual rights to life, liberty, and property that people agreed to form and submit to a government. And because according to him, everyone was born equal and free, so a government needed each person's consent to be truly legitimate.

Yet another caveat to the government's rule was that it was applicable only to the outward actions of the citizen: in other words, a man's conscience was private. And this exception would form the basis of Locke's advocacy of the separation of religious and political authority or separation of the Church and the State.

RIGHT OF REBELLION

Even more significant was Locke's ideas on the rights of citizens to rise up against a tyrannical government. This was a highly revolutionary and potentially dangerous idea since the one person who had written something similar—Algernon Sidney in his *Discourses Concerning Government*—had been arrested and executed for treason. And although the sixteenth-century protestant reformer John Calvin had accepted that tyrants should be brought down, he had prohibited ordinary people from using this option. Instead, he had empowered only magistrates with the task.

In complete departure from the Hobbesian position of complete obedience to the sovereign ruler, Locke argued that if the legislature changed its form against the will of the majority, or if it was suspended or abolished by the executive, then the legislative body, as people knew it, was adequately altered and could be dissolved. This would release the citizens from their original contract who would be 'at liberty to provide for themselves...by erecting a new legislative.' However, Locke went on to warn against indiscriminate use of this clause to mount rebellions as it would lead to anarchy in society.

PRIVATE PROPERTY

Other major themes of Locke's *Second Treatise* were Property and Labour. Again, unlike the Hobbesian notion of the state coming into existence first and then property, Locke regarded private property as existing before and being the rationale for the formation of the state. He also argued that it was not nature but human labour that almost always was the ultimate source of value. Things existing in the natural state usually had little or no value; it was the addition of labour and the creation of goods that led to the creation or increase in value. This idea served as the launch pad for his labour theory of property, according to which it was the application of labour to a natural resource that changed it into a property and hence, determined ownership. This was also how Locke explained private ownership in the face of arguments that questioned personal claim to earth's resources if the earth was created by God. According to Locke, since man owned himself and thus, his labour, any resource to which he added his labour could be grounds for private property. However, he added a Proviso according to which, appropriation of un-owned resources was acceptable only as long as it did not make anyone worse off than what they would have been before.

RIGHTS OF MAN

As important as Locke's theory of property was in the economic perspective, its corollary held even greater significance for political philosophy. The idea that man owned himself further underlined his political liberalism and the right of the citizen to offer or withdraw his consent to the government through the social contract. Additionally, one of the main reasons for the creation of governments was the protection of private property which was also why the state could not arbitrarily dispose of property.

Locke also wrote several essays like the *Essay Concerning Human Understanding*, *The Reasonableness of Christianity* and *Some Thoughts Concerning Education* as well as public Letters like *A Letter Concerning Toleration*. These generally spoke in favour of separation of ecclesiastical and civil authority as well as legal tolerance for religious differences. This was hardly surprising since in the wake of 1683, after a failed assassination attempt on King Charles II, nicknamed the Rye House Plot, Locke found himself accused of treason and had to flee England. It was only with the Glorious Revolution of 1688 that enthroned William III (of Orange) as the King of England and the establishment of Protestantism as the official religion that religious and political strife lessened. In 1688, Locke returned to England and got his works published.

LATER YEARS AND LEGACY

The political ascension of the Whigs and Protestantism after the Glorious Revolution meant that Locke was viewed with great regard not only in the political circles but also as a philosopher, scientist and writer. However, with advancing age, his health began to suffer which is why he moved to Essex. There, he finally passed away on 28 October 1704.

John Locke's concept of social contract, built on the foundation stone of the concepts of individual liberty and equality, impacted almost all corners of the world. While the leaders of American Revolution of 1776, like Jefferson, and those of the French Revolution of 1789, like Voltaire, were inspired directly, eventually anti-establishment struggles in

European colonies across Asia and Africa took inspiration from Locke's arguments for the rights of man.

> ### «KNOW MORE»
>
> - As the chief physician of Lord Anthony Ashley Cooper, the First Earl of Shaftesbury, John Locke recommended surgery when the latter was gravely ill with an abscess in the liver. The nobleman survived the surgery–itself a life-threatening procedure in those times–and credited Locke for saving his life.
> - Locke had a long and close friendship with Damaris Masham, the wife of Sir Francis Masham. She was 26 years younger to him and Locke admired her intellect and her spirit of curiosity. He died in her Essex family home, reportedly as she was reading the Psalms to him.

11

MONTESQUIEU

Baron de Montesquieu, father of modern political theory, figures in many academic curricula of the world in present-day. A quintessential figure of the Age of Enlightenment in Europe, Montesquieu was a French nobleman and thinker whose *Spirit of Laws* turned out to be a seminal work of political philosophy and influenced the drafting of the American Declaration of Independence, among other works of political significance.

EARLY LIFE

Born as Charles-Louis de Secondat on 18 January 1689 at the Château La Brède, near Bordeaux in France, the future political theorist grew up in an aristocratic family that owned fertile wine-producing estates. While his father, Jacques de Secondat, could trace his lineage to an old family name that had distinguished itself in the service of the Crown as far back as the sixteenth century, his mother Marie-Françoise de Pesnel was of partial English ancestry who had brought a considerable dowry of land into the family. Unfortunately, she died when Charles-Louis was only seven, but as her oldest son, he was left the barony of La Brède which went a long way in ensuring for him a comfortable education.

Young Charles-Louis was sent to be educated in Collège de Juilly near Paris after which he enrolled into the University of Bordeaux to study law. Upon graduating in 1708, he moved to Paris with the intention of practicing law as an advocate but had to return to Bordeaux in 1713 after his father's death.

However, a series of family events turned out to be more fortunate for Charles-Louis—the first among these was his wedding to a lady named Jeanne de Lartigue from a wealthy family and the other was the death of his uncle, Jean-Baptiste in 1716, as a result of which he inherited the latter's estates along with the barony of Montesquieu, near Agen, as well as the office of deputy president in the Parlement of Bordeaux. Thus, at twenty-seven years of age, Charles-Louis was not only assured of financial comfort for life but more importantly, the official appointment marked the beginning of his engagement with civic and political matters of the day.

PERSIAN LETTERS

In 1722, Montesquieu anonymously published a witty satire on contemporary French life, especially the Parisian society. Titled *Persian Letters*, it was written as an epistolary novel in the voice of two Persian travellers who travel across France during the reign of Louis XIV and note the political, religious and economic institutions of the land. The work was an irreverent attack on Roman Catholic superstitions as well as the vanities of the Parisian court. At a deeper level though, it dealt with matters like many fundamental differences between European and Oriental cultures, Christianity and Islam, besides offering acute comparisons of different forms of governments and social systems as well as the bleak realization that it was impossible for a man to achieve full self-knowledge.

TRAVELS AND EARLY WORKS

The book brought Montesquieu both literary fame and social attention which he was able to use to get a foothold in courtly society. He decided to sell his official appointment at Bordeaux and in 1728, eventually, managed to secure his living in Paris by acquiring a position in the Academie Francaise with a little help from his new, well-connected Parisian friends. The matter of livelihood now settled, Montesquieu decided to see more of different countries and cultures in Europe and over the next three years, he travelled across Austria, Hungary, Italy, Germany and Holland. He ended his tour in England where he actively engaged with the political culture of the time.

Montesquieu's extensive travels had made him hungry to get back to pen and paper. After his return to France, he made straight for his estate at La Brede rather than linger over the pleasures of Paris. Writing furiously over a period of two years, he produced a short-lived treatise on the French monarchy titled *La Monarchie Universelle* which, because of the ensuing controversy, he decided to withdraw almost immediately after its publication in 1734. The other work from this time was a history of the Roman Empire titled *Reflections on the Causes of the Grandeur and Declension of the Romans*. In this, he gave one of the first indications of his horror of despotism, showing how the military might and wealth of Rome merely led to tyrannical rulers and weakening of the spirit of civic virtues in the Roman citizens. Like in the *Persian Letters*, Montesquieu once again described Non-European civilizations like the Byzantine and Ottoman, this time with regard to the impact of the disintegrating Roman Empire.

SPIRIT OF LAWS

Montesquieu was, however, far from satisfied with his historical work; taking shape in his mind was an ambitious project that would offer a comprehensive account of the origin, meanings, types and functions of laws across social systems. To prepare for this, he started reading voraciously and filling huge volumes with notes. When his eyesight began to fail, he employed secretaries, clerks and amanuensis to finish books ranging from law and political theory to history and economics. Finally, after almost eight years of research, writing, revisions and editing, the book was published in 1748 under the title *Spirit of Laws* with another edition issued in 1750.

Over 1036 pages that made up 31 books and two volumes, the book explained the working of laws in various socio-political systems. According to Montesquieu, it was not enough to understand the origin of law as a way of regulating social life but it was necessary to put it in the lived context. He believed that to understand a particular group of people and their laws, one had to look at their geography, climate, economy, religion, culture, customs and practices.

Later critics often found fault with Montesquieu's doctrine of the political influence of climate which related the physical conditions of people to their 'general spirit'. However, except in cases of what he termed 'primitive cultures', he never insisted that human beings could not rise above this physical influence. He asserted instead that it was the lawmaker's duty in societies to counteract it and thereby, help the civilization to evolve.

PHILOSOPHY OF LAWS

A further example of his practical approach to laws was to warn against misguided attempts to reform systems that had generally proved to be functional. For example, if a monarch decided to change the laws of his land and weaken the nobility with the ultimate aim of strengthening his own throne, then the resulting political system would lead to despotism, leading to instability and destruction. However, this did not mean Montesquieu thought that the purpose of laws was to maintain status-quo; instead, he believed that a true understanding of the relation between the laws and the fundamental principles of society would actually allow lawmakers to pave the way for reforms and a more progressive society. Among such reforms that Montesquieu thought monarchs could bring about were the abolition of slavery, ceasing of religious persecution and, essentially, making governance less arbitrary and complex.

Montesquieu was a firm believer in the simplicity and

directness of laws; according to him, laws of a society should be concerned only with the most pressing matters—the safety of its citizens and keeping of public order–rather than religion and customs. He came up with a, typically, witty example to make his point saying that there was no need for laws to deal with offenses against God since He did not require their protection. More significantly though, this formed the basis of his argument in favour of separating law and religion, thereby, bolstering theoretical foundations of secular law.

Montesquieu also illustrated the fallacy of making laws that prohibited actions which people might perform inadvertently like bumping into a statue of a saint or king. He essentially said that laws should neither be too many nor too vague since then the focus was no longer on ensuring justice but more on finding fault. The whole point of making laws should be to help citizens avoid committing crimes in the first place and, thereby, make it easier for them to avoid punishment.

FORMS OF GOVERNMENT

The main reason why *Spirit of Laws* figures as a seminal work on political philosophy today is because of Montesquieu's explication firstly, of forms of government and secondly, of the necessity of separation of powers. In dealing with the former, Montesquieu gave up the classical three-fold classification of governments into monarchy, aristocracy, and democracy. He, instead, categorized governments as monarchy, despotic and republican which, in turn, could be democratic or aristocratic. Each form of government owed its existence to a founding principle – 'human passions which set it in motion' – and corruption of this principle could lead to the destruction of the corresponding form of government. Thus, for a republic, this principle was virtue; for monarchy, it was honour while despotism functioned on fear.

Another way that Montesquieu differed from the classicists was that he did not differentiate between monarchy and aristocracy on the basis of virtue of the sovereign—a distinction made famous by Aristotle in his *Ethics*. Instead, the Frenchman explained that when the sovereign ruled according to 'fixed and established laws', it was a monarchy but when he did not, it turned into despotism. In a monarchy, though the king was sovereign, the actual governance was executed through institutions like subordinate nobility and an independent judiciary. In contrast, despotism was marked by the destruction of these institutions for the sole aim of increasing the power and wealth of the ruler. In the end, though, despotism turned out to be more unstable since fear and suspicion became the underlying principles of such a government. A monarchy, on the other hand, functioned smoothly because of the principle of honour according to which the upright action of a subject was proportionately rewarded. Thus, when a monarch started ruling unfairly— rewarding for shameful behaviour rather than for virtue—then he broke the correlation between honour and conduct and paved the way for despotism.

A democracy, Montesquieu explained, was the rule of the people – whether the government was run by elected ministers or on the advice of the senate, it was the citizens who chose them. The underlying principle of democracy was political virtue which made citizens put public good ahead of personal interest. Montesquieu was too much of a realist to note that such virtue did not come, naturally, to humans. He believed that democracy needed to be sustained by education so that people knew the importance of equating personal well-being with broader national and civic welfare. Additionally, such political virtues had to be protected by legal institutions so that public wealth was safeguarded and equitable distribution of resources in society was encouraged.

Montesquieu identified two ways that could corrupt democratic principles; the first by 'spirit of inequality' which would lead certain people to amass huge wealth and political power over others and hence break down the identification between public welfare and personal interest. The second was the complete opposite 'spirit of too much equality' which would do away with all rational, legal authorities and hence, reduce society to chaos and mob rule–eventually, the strongest anarchist among them will replace the fallen democracy with despotism.

Aristocracy was defined by Montesquieu as that form of government in which one section of the society ruled over the rest. The underlying principle of this system was moderation since an excessive accumulation of wealth or political power would result in the ruling elite becoming despots. Thus, in an aristocracy, it was extremely important that the principle of moderation be protected by certain legal checks like denying the aristocrats the right to impose taxes as well as a culture of simple living. Furthermore, there should be equality among the aristocrats themselves so that no single person was allowed to become more powerful than others.

SEPARATION OF POWERS

Apart from an elaboration on the various forms of laws and governments, the other significant subject in Montesquieu's *Spirit of Laws* is the separation of powers. He strongly advocated that the legislative, executive and judiciary be allowed distinct areas of function. According to Montesquieu, the separation of powers formed the fundamental condition of political liberty, without which society would become vulnerable to despotism. Thus, if the same person made laws and executed them, his governance would be arbitrary and tyrannical. Likewise, if judiciary and executive were merged, then equality before the law would suffer and liberty too would be compromised. It was only when the three arms of the state were separated that they could act as a check on each other and ensure just and liberal governance.

Montesquieu ended the *Spirit of Laws* by tracing the evolution of French law, its division into written and customary law along with an investigation into the origins of the aristocracy in France. The immense scholarly effort that went into the massive tome gained him appreciation from different parts of the continent and even across the Atlantic where it turned out to be a major influence on America's *Declaration of Independence* as well as its Constitution.

LATER LIFE

Some institutions like the Church attacked the *Spirit of Laws* and in 1750, Montesquieu published a *Defence* to answer his critics. Towards the end of his life, Diderot and D'Alembert requested him to write a piece for the *Encyclopaedia* and Montesquieu, with his usual penchant for the unexpected, agreed to write an *Essay on Taste*. But before he could finish the work, he died in Paris in 1755.

«KNOW MORE»

- Montesquieu admired his wife's business acumen and left her in charge of his country estates during long periods of residence in Paris.
- During his visit to England, Montesquieu was requested by Prince of Wales to make an anthology of French songs.

12

JEAN-JACQUES ROUSSEAU

Jean-Jacques Rousseau was a French thinker and philosopher of the Age of Enlightenment. His political theories, of a social contract and general will, as well as developmental ideas like the importance of psychological autonomy, influenced not only concrete historical events including the French Revolution but generations of later writers, artists and leaders across the world.

EARLY LIFE

Born on 28 June 1712 in the Swiss city of Geneva, Rousseau lost his mother during his birth and had an unpredictable childhood. During his initial years, his father brought him up who then got into trouble with the law and fled the city. Young Rousseau was then taken care of by relatives on his mother's side who never lost an opportunity to remind the boy of his unfortunate circumstances. Fed up with constant humiliation, Rousseau ran away when he was just 16 years old and after wandering through Sardinia and then France, finally arrived in Savoy. There, finally, fortune smiled on him as he became a steward to a noblewoman, Baroness de Warens, who not only gave him employment but also supervised his education and transformation into a refined man of letters.

SUCCESS IN PARIS

Soon though, Rousseau was tired of playing protégé and lover to a rich woman and made his way to Paris where he befriended another adventurous and intelligent man, Denis Diderot. The mid-eighteenth century was an exciting time in the French capital–thanks to Voltaire's progressive writings, revolution was in the air and soon, Rousseau joined a group of young and radical intellectuals known as 'Philosophes' who initiated literary and scientific enterprises as the *Encylopedie* with the goal of popularizing secular, scientific and liberal temperament among the literate population of France. Such was the magnetism of Rousseau's liberal and artistic energy that he also composed operas of which the, *Le Devin du village* or *The Village Soothsayer* of 1752, received adulation from the reigning King Louis XV. He would also go on to attain fame as a novelist with his *Julie, ou la nouvelle Héloïse* in 1761. This turned out to be one of the bestselling fictional works of the eighteenth century and also contributed to the development of Romanticism. Rousseau would also be one of the earliest writers of the autobiographical genre. Though St Augustine had written his *Confessions*, about his spiritual journey, way back in the Middle Ages, Rousseau's *The Confessions* completed in 1770, on the other hand, was about his entire life including the scandals, repentance, triumphs and nostalgia.

PHILOSOPHY OF HUMAN KNOWLEDGE

Rousseau had other fires burning in him and, soon, he started putting his highly original and powerful ideas to paper. One of his earliest philosophical works was *A Discourse on the Sciences and the Arts written in* 1750 in which, for the first time, appeared his central tenet that the history of Western civilization is one of decay and corruption. Rousseau believed that in the original, natural scheme of things, humans were good and pure but increasing sophistication of civilization had only led to decadence and harm.

For a brief while, Rousseau's liberal philosophical energies were directed against French composer Jean-Philippe Rameau who represented the tradition and convention in the musical arts of the times. By championing the cause of melody over harmony as Rameau did, Rousseau paved the way for one of the core ideas of Romanticism–that spontaneous creative expression was superior to slavish adherence to rules and decorum.

THEORY OF INEQUALITY

Tired of the old debates in France, Rousseau returned to Geneva where he started work on his second major philosophical treatise—Discourse on the Origin of Inequality. In this, he propounded that human inequality was of two types. The first was the result of natural differences in strength, intellect, appearance and so on. The second, that he termed 'moral inequality', was imposed by humans on each other in the form of social practices and institutions.

Originally, humans led isolated lives, they were differentiated from animals by their capacity for free will, a fundamental orientation towards self-care that he termed 'amour de soi' and even a natural tendency to feel compassion or pity. In this way, mankind, in the beginning, lived in a free and pure state. But with progressing civilization, mankind developed a kind of artificial pride, the 'amour-propre' compelling humans to compare themselves with each other. This, in turn, not only led to feelings of insecurity and fear but also to seeking pleasure in the pain or weakness of others. In this way, the desire for positive regard from others while, on one hand, encouraged economic development like agriculture, metallurgy as well as private property and the division of labour, it also led to inequality as people strived to acquire control or superiority over others.

THEORY OF SOCIAL CONTRACT

The role played by property in Rousseau's 'Theory of Inequality' made up the cornerstone of his political philosophy. He argued that ownership of property by humans led to immorality borne out of jealousy and anger. More importantly, it led to social inequality and made necessary the formation of laws and governments which led to further corruption. In this context, he also criticized the social contract theory, pointing out that the resulting political arrangement was heavily biased in favour of the rich and the powerful.

All this came in for more detailed treatment in his seminal work of political philosophy, The Social Contract that was published in 1762. The book opens with one of the most dramatic lines in philosophy, 'Man is born free and everywhere he is in chains.' It was because of the coercive laws and institutions, which characterized the common form of social contract, that mankind found itself bound and oppressed.

In his book, Rousseau went further than the flaws of the social contract to come up with ways on how mankind could regain its liberty in the times to come. And he found one of the models of a healthier socio-political system in his adopted city-state–Geneva— that he praised for having acquired the balance between 'the equality which nature established among men and the inequality which they have instituted among themselves.'

GENERAL WILL

Far more influential in *The Social Contract*, however, was his 'Theory of General Will' which, according to Rousseau, united citizens of a truly civil society. The General Will was that of the sovereign, or all the people together, that aimed for the common good. In such a system, individuals could achieve both self-preservation as well as liberty. This was because acceptance of the authority of the general will of the people as a whole would protect individuals from being subordinated to the will of specific individuals. It would also ensure that they themselves obeyed the law as, collectively, they were the authors of the law.

Rousseau recognized that the general will could sometimes come into conflict with personal interest but its ultimate purpose was to further the public or national interest, common to all. It was also the general will which brought a Republic in existence. This was, according to Rousseau, the fairest kind of social contract, characterized by the surrender of unhealthy personal rights by the citizens–like those based on brute strength– in return for civil rights based on liberalism and true equality. This general will also made for true law that was just and willingly obeyed by all citizens unlike actual laws in operation which were made to continue with arbitrary, unequal privileges to certain classes.

VIEWS ON EDUCATION

It was not long before Rousseau felt a yearning to return to France but this time, he decided to live in a secluded country cottage in accordance with his philosophy of the ideal life being close to Nature. However, the publication of his book *Emile, or On Education* caused a furore because of its advocacy of highly unconventional ways of bringing up children which did not exclude deceit and mental cruelty. Though his last work, *The New Eloise,* appearing as fiction, escaped much of *Emile*'s fate, Rousseau, eventually, had to escape France to avoid imprisonment.

DEATH AND LEGACY

After a brief stay in London, Rousseau returned to France and found a measure of peace at last. He married his long-time partner, Therese, and produced a series of autobiographical works in which he explained or justified his earlier controversial writings. Towards the end of his life, Rousseau also regained some degree of political patronage as he died at Ermonville, the country estate of Marquis de Girardin after suffering a haemorrhage on 2 July 1778. After sixteen years, his remains were finally taken to the Pantheon in Paris and laid to rest in a grave that stood across from his more accepted contemporary, Voltaire.

Rousseau's influence on the history of Western thought, politics, culture and arts can hardly be overemphasized. Though his views on the education of women—to make men's lives 'easy and agreeable' would come to be heavily criticized by feminists, his theories on creativity and the guidance available in Nature rang the death knell for Classicism and ushered in the full flowering of Romanticism in art, literature and culture across the continent. Politically, his ideas on liberalism and general will inspired the leaders of the French Revolution while those on property and laws influenced later ideologies like Marxism and Socialism.

> ## «KNOW MORE»
>
> - Rousseau's partiality towards masochism and exhibitionism in adult life has been traced back to the experience of corporal punishment during his childhood at the hands of the pastor's sister in Geneva.
> - Since Rousseau was allowed to return to Paris in 1770 on the condition that he would not publish any books, towards the end of his life, he partially made a living by copying music. Today, however, his fame has witnessed a popular revival. The French town of Ermonville, where Rousseau breathed his last, now hosts a festival in his memory replete with fireworks, live entertainment and a 'citizens' banquet', including champagne, two kinds of wines as well as Rousseau-inspired main course dishes.

13

EDMUND BURKE

Edmund Burke was among the most influential political thinkers of the 'Age of Enlightenment' in Britain. His long experience of almost 20 years as a parliamentarian led him to ground his views in statecraft and political life in specific and lived traditions and practices, rather than in mere abstract theories. Burke's writings were especially influential in the American War of Independence as they steered British politics away from the extremes of the French Revolution.

EARLY LIFE

Edmund Burke was born in Dublin in 1729 into a professional and well-to-do family. His father was a solicitor and for a time, even young Edmund toyed with the idea of taking the law as a profession. Of greater significance was his upbringing in a mixed religious environment. While his father was a Protestant, his mother was a Catholic and for a time, he studied in a boarding school run by Quakers. It was, however, his years at Dublin's Trinity College which provided him an expansive education, not only in the ancients—Homer, Cicero, Virgil, Sallust, Juvenal, Xenophon, Lucian and Epictetus—but also in English greats such as Milton and Shakespeare. Burke's philosophical leanings were evident in a treatise that he started writing during this time in college, titled *A Philosophical Enquiry into the Origin of Our Ideas of the Sublime and Beautiful* but which would be published much later in 1757. By this time, he was in London and trying to make a living from writing about the political matters of the day. His major work from this time was *A Vindication of Natural Society* which was published anonymously in 1756 and can be regarded as, perhaps, the first serious defence of Anarchism, though later for the sake of a government appointment, he would characterize it as a satire. Nevertheless, the treatise would go on to influence later anarchists like William Godwin. In this work, he attacked one of the Enlightenment's most favourite fancies about the value of living in a pre-civil 'natural state'—the kind of philosophy that was popularized by Rousseau and supported in Britain by Tory official and philosopher, Lord Bolingbroke. Burke, instead, believed that it was living in 'little platoons' or institutions like a family, the church and the local community that really inculcated virtues such as temperance and fortitude in human beings. Living in the local and particular context, mankind was able to embody the ideal civic life.

TIMES OF FLUX

The mid-eighteenth century was a time of rapid political and economic changes in Britain. The lack of strong leadership from the Crown had raised the spectre of regency while anarchy was looming in France in the form of the French Revolution. Added to these fluctuations was the ferment in socio-economic conditions in the English society. Growing wealth had made the middle-class vocal in their demands for a share in the governance of the country. At the same time, a broadening oligarchy had realized the need for a more frequent collaboration of public opinion. In general, common confidence in the discussion and power of conviction was seen across Europe.

POLITICAL INITIATIVES

Not surprisingly then in 1765, Burke decided to join politics. With the help of his patron Lord Rockingham, he became a member of the British Parliament wherein he was a powerful voice in the debates over the limits of royal authority. As a member of the Parliament, Burke advocated parliamentary control over royal expenditure as well as patronage. With the passage of the Stamp Act in the same year, Burke foresaw the trouble that such harsh economic colonial laws would bring to Britain. Burke was a statesman, capable of the shrewdest and deepest views; he owed his intuitive power to his strong sense of realities and to his knowledge of mankind. His exact judgement regarding the possible issues of the American discontent came from his understanding of the deepest motives which had led the colonies to revolt. As the American opposition to the unfair Stamp Act grew,

Burke counselled for pragmatism and moderation in dealing with the colonies. Fortunately, Lord Rockingham's short-lived government was able to repeal the Stamp Act but even when the faction still found itself in the opposition, Burke continued to point out the flaws of Britain's violent opposition to American Independence. He, in fact, suggested that the American states, which wanted to cede from the British Crown, be allowed to do so peacefully.

Likewise, Burke also brought attention to the excessively exploitive governance in one of Britain's biggest colonies—India. He suggested that the colonial government should respect local traditions and practices besides putting an end to patronage from interested parties. Though his proposal which said that India should be governed by independent commissioners in London was defeated but eventually, the spotlight on the extent of colonial loot in India led to the trial of former Governor-General of Bengal, Warren Hastings. Burke argued that Hastings had proved to be a 'captain-general of iniquity' who never dined without 'creating a famine'. Burke emphasized that, based on the principles of the natural order and divine law, there needed to be limits even to the empire's imposition in the colonies.

All such views on Britain's colonial policies found expression in Burke's *Thoughts on the Cause of the Present Discontents,* published in 1770. In the colonies, he advocated a kind of government based on a more cooperative and practical relationship between the rulers and the subjects rather than a blind, absolutist adherence to the colonizer's power. Most significantly, his notion of colonial governance was rooted in a particular time and place rather than bound to abstract notions of rule and authority. Thus, instead of debating whether the British Parliament was right or wrong in imposing its rule over colonial subjects, Burke pointed out that it was in Britain's interest to keep its subjects happy. Rather than insisting on its rights to put down the rebellion in the colonies, Britain would do better if it accorded dignity and justice to its subjects.

The same pragmatic approach was to recur in Burke's famous opposition to the French Revolution expressed with force and reason under the title, *Reflections on the Revolution in France* published in 1790. In this, he pointed out the dangers inherent in theoretical concepts like 'The Rights of Man' which could lead to arbitrary interpretations that can be used to overturn social systems which had been functioning for ages. Rather than using mere abstractions to enforce social and political changes, Burke believed that one had to first truly understand the limitations imposed by the existing conditions and then usher gradual improvements. In fact, through his warnings, Burke anticipated the worst excesses of Jacobin violence in France of the 1790s. Burke's economic views would also come to influence later thinkers. He advocated a free market system and advised governments to stay away from the economy unless absolutely necessary. However, he cautioned that the free market would only benefit society when the trade was fair and open to all. Also, Burke was less than enthusiastic about large-scale industrialization, foreseeing the destruction of the traditional ways of life.

DEATH AND LEGACY

Burke's defence of prudence and tradition at the height of the French Revolution was far from popular even in Britain and provoked responses such as *The Rights of Man* eloquently argued by younger thinkers like Thomas Paine. Also, his last days were darkened by personal unhappiness caused by the death of his only son. Burke retired from the parliament in 1794 and though he was offered the title of Lord Beaconsfield, he declined it in favour of a generous pension. Burke spent the final years of his life writing to defend British virtues of tradition, rank and property.

Burke's political views eventually came to guide British foreign policy based on reason and caution. He took British conservatism out of the nebulous regions of pre-conceived ideas and let them gain strength under the full light of open discussion. All the political ideas of the Conservatives and the Traditionalists can be traced back to the teachings of Burke. In fact, Legouis and Cazamian in *The History of English Literature* go so far as to write that 'Disraeli's real master was Burke, and no other.'

Though detractors accused him of conservatism and orthodoxy, Burke always believed in the necessity of adaptability. If with time, he revealed changes in some of his ideas, it was not because of any unprincipled fluctuations in character, but rather because he believed one had to keep up with life—its twists and turns. First a Whig, then a Tory; at one time, the supporter of constitutional liberties and then the opposer of the French Revolution—for Burke, all were complementary attitudes of one and the same personality. He believed that though the past had its value, it was equally important to recognize that change is inevitable and can, hopefully, lead to new opportunities for the reaffirmation of traditional values.

«KNOW MORE»

- In 1782, for a brief while, Burke was appointed the Paymaster of Forces and Privy Counsellor. In the latter appointment, he succeeded in abolishing 134 offices in the royal household and civil administration to prevent wasteful expenditure.
- Burke originally intended *Reflections on the Revolution in France* to be written as a letter to a Frenchman.

14

IMMANUEL KANT

One of the greatest philosophers in the world, Immanuel Kant left a lasting impact on the study of ethics, metaphysics, aesthetics and political theory in the history of Western civilization. Best known for his critical series that include *Critique of Pure Reason, Critique of Practical Reason* as well as *Critique of Judgement*, his works reveal a deep entwining of moral and political philosophy.

EARLY LIFE

Immanuel Kant was born on 22 April 1724 in the then Prussian city of Königsberg which is now known as Kaliningrad in present-day Russia. As his father was a harness maker, young Immanuel grew up in modest circumstances but his intellectual prowess was never in doubt. When he was just sixteen, he started studying theology, physics and mathematics at the University of Königsberg. Unfortunately, the untimely death of his father meant that young Kant could no longer afford to pay for his studies and had to leave the university. Though he soon managed to get a position as a private tutor to the children of wealthy families, his heart was in academics. In 1755, he was able to return to the university to pursue his studies and went on to earn his doctorate. Though over the next decade, he had to work hard in an unsalaried position as a private docent, Kant wrote several papers during this time on metaphysics and logic.

The most important work by Kant in these years was *Critique of Pure Reason* which was actually a response to the contemporary philosophical divide between rationalists like Leibnitz and empiricists like David Hume. While the former believed that the only objective way to understand the world was by Reason, the latter put forward the impossibility of understanding anything independent of Experience. Kant's work sought to find a middle ground between these two extremes by pointing out that by studying the way human understanding structures all experiences, it was possible to arrive at general conclusions about the material world. This notion of the human mind organizing experiences with the purpose of understanding how the world works turned out to be a milestone in the study of Western metaphysics and epistemology.

THEORY OF CATEGORICAL IMPERATIVE

In 1770, Kant was invited to a full-fledged academic position in the University of Königsberg where he became a professor of metaphysics and logic. With financial worries out of the way, Kant was able to devote all his energies to his philosophical work. Yet another major theme of his writings was the philosophy of morality, best expressed in his theory of the 'categorical imperative'. According to this, morality was the logical consequence of Reason and all moral actions could be rationally explained. Hence, there was no grey area between right and wrong and it was crucial for mankind to believe in this imperative order to lead a truly moral life.

This concern with morality also informed about Kant's political philosophy and the two were linked by the notion of free will. Kant believed that unless human beings had the freedom to act immorally, their virtuous actions could not be considered truly moral. Moreover, each person was equipped with a conscience that helped him to recognize the authority of the moral laws. Known as a 'fact of reason,' this notion served as the basis of Kant's belief in human freedom. And yet this freedom did not imply that the individual was at liberty to do as he pleased—in which case, he was not really free. Instead, it was only by acting morally, could he truly act autonomously since then he was acting according to the moral law he had given himself and not merely following virtuous action based on others' desires.

POLITICAL THOUGHT

It was this notion of human autonomy at the heart of morality, which also determined political activity. In one of his earliest political writings, the 1793 essay, 'On the Old Saw: That May Be Right in Theory, But It Won't Work in Practice', Kant reflected on the supposed contradiction between theory and practice faced by human beings throughout their lives. He treated this conundrum in three different contexts starting from the personal to political and finally, international. First, he considered the dilemma of the common man when confronted by a choice between moral and practical action. Next, he discussed the predicament of the politician with regard to the limits of political obligation and finally, of the global citizen whose actions could well determine the difference between war and peace among nations.

At the very beginning, Kant made it clear that in his scheme of things, there was no conflict between the moral requirements of an action and its practical possibilities. While earlier philosophers like Hobbes had gone on to explain civil society as a way of curbing innate human irrationality, Kant believed that only the civil state offered mankind the opportunity to fulfil their human destiny. Thus, to be truly human meant living in a civil state. However, he also realized that to bring about such a condition, the state had to be secured only by the law. In the end, the essay explored the difficulties of ensuring peace among nations guided only by self-interest and greed for power. Such a mountainous task could be achieved, Kant recognized only by establishing strict international laws, which could never be formulated or implemented if one was too mindful of the prevalent harsh realities—rather they (the laws) had to be based on theory.

THE RECHTSSTAAT

Kant returned to the topic of laws and state in his major

political works, *Project for a Perpetual Peace* published in 1795 and *Metaphysics of Morals* published in 1797. Unlike the Renaissance political writer Machiavelli, Kant was firm that political success could be achieved independently of moral laws. He believed that the ideal state could only be based on the rule of law or Rechtsstaat. This was because, according to him, only a constitutional state governed by law would protect the civic freedom and dignity of its citizens. He termed such a state as a 'republic' which held the written constitution above all else, where the executive and legislative were separated unlike 'despotisms' where the law was determined by a single person and hence, was no longer universal. Interestingly, he considered democracy as a variation of a similar kind of despotism, since in those times, the term implied direct democracy as opposed to representative democracy of today. Kant feared that in such a democracy where people directly took decisions on political matters and made laws (direct democracy), the majority rule would inevitably threaten individual liberty.

He further elaborated his theory of classical republicanism in *The Doctrine of Rights* which was published as first part of *The Metaphysics of the Morals* in 1785 and then separately in 1797. In this work, Kant went further than other social contract theorists in stating that it was not just a matter of self-interest which made human beings enter the contract with a state; rather it was a matter of respecting universal human freedom which made it obligatory on the part of human beings to create a Rechtssaat if it did not exist already.

And yet for all his belief in freedom and autonomy, Kant

did not advocate outright rebellion even in cases where governments failed to protect the rights of its citizens. This is because Kant saw the right to the revolution not only leading to anarchy but irrational too since governments embodied the universal law of the right. Kant suggested that people speak out against corrupt governments by the use of public reason. In international affairs too, Kant recognized this tension between principle and reality. Though he believed that a state of permanent peace was a moral imperative, this could come about only if a set of improbable conditions were met. Such conditions which he elaborated in *Project for a Perpetual Peace* included the founding of constitutional republics throughout the world, strengthening of the political community, disbanding of armies by the republics thus formed, never incurring debt and so on. Though the possibility of states meeting such conditions seemed far-fetched, yet precisely in the interests of self-preservation and profit, they may, eventually, agree to a mechanism to avoid war and promote peace which, in the Kantian worldview, is a moral imperative.

An interesting feature of Kant's political philosophy was the upholding of the university as a space where creative ideas can be discussed. The figure of the academician-philosopher was crucial in this context as he was the one to guide in the development of subjects like theology, law and medicine in accordance with Reason. Kant also believed that the state would be better governed if its leader allowed himself to be guided by the counsel of such a philosopher-teacher figure.

DEATH AND LEGACY

Kant continued to teach and write into the 1790s. However, at the turn of the century, his memory began to fail and at the age of 80, in 1804, Kant passed away.

Kant's writings on ethics, aesthetics, metaphysics and politics comprise of a formidable corpus of philosophical work which not only provided direction to German thought for several decades to come, as became evident in the works of Marx and Nietzsche, but also went on to influence other philosophers like Michel Foucault and statesmen like Woodrow Wilson with the idea of the 'League of Nations'. Kant's tomb in the cathedral of Königsberg remains inscribed with words which bear testimony to his abiding concerns of metaphysics and ethics—'the starry heavens above me and moral law within me'.

«KNOW MORE»

- Kant was so regular with his afternoon walks that the citizens of Königsberg could set their clocks according to his position on the street.
- Kant lived and died in the city where he was born—Königsberg—and throughout his life, never travelled more than forty miles beyond.

15

MARY WOLLSTONECRAFT

Self-titled, 'dissenting spirit', Mary Wollstonecraft was a writer, activist, social reformer and political philosopher who is best remembered today for *A Vindication Of The Rights Of Women*—a passionate advocacy of women's education on modern lines at par with men. Apart from treatises, she also wrote novels, pamphlets, translations, travelogues and critical reviews on historical and political subjects as well as varied aspects of philosophy.

EARLY LIFE

Mary Wollstonecraft was born on 27 April 1759 in Spitalfields, London. Growing up as the second of seven children in a family of modest means, Mary had to shoulder domestic responsibilities early on. The social pretensions of a father who had frittered away a considerable legacy of his children in his fruitless desire to become a gentleman farmer did not help matters. Mary's childhood was punctuated by several relocations in search of affordable living conditions.

Growing up as a daughter in a family of limited means also meant that Mary's education was not a priority. What she, eventually, learned was picked up over erratic periods of schooling and her own reading of the *Bible*, classical philosophers as well as English writers like Shakespeare and Milton. Among her siblings, only the oldest, a son, received formal education and eventually, he also went on to be the sole claimant of their grandfather's legacy. Not surprisingly, such discrimination against the girls, and its unfortunate consequences, including her sisters suffering from depression, failed marriages and financial need, would rankle Mary through her growing years and intensify her sense of injustice against women.

At the age of nineteen, Mary was forced to take up a job as a lady's companion but had to leave let it go after three years on account of her mother's illness. A series of family tragedies followed, including the death of Mrs Wollstonecraft, the breakdown of her sister's marriage and their rejection by other members of the family. Inspired by the moral and political reformist views of Reverend Richard Price, Mary decided to move to Newington to be a part of the progressive community of Dissenters. She even set-up a school there to give shape to her dreams of girls' education, but a far more useful result of the association was an introduction to a London publisher of radical books, Joseph Johnson.

EARLY WORKS

Johnson agreed to publish Wollstonecraft's first major work,

Thoughts on the Education of Daughters: With Reflections on Female Conduct in the more Important Duties of Life in 1787. In this work, she called upon parents and guardians of society to allow education of girls so that their natural institutions and emotions could be governed and strengthened by Reason. The disjuncture between Reason and Emotion was an old one that had enjoyed a period of resurgence in the Age of Pope and Neo-classicists. Wollstonecraft pointed out the way women had been unfairly deprived of the benefits of Reason and its use in education. She was astute enough not to pitch the demand for female educational reform as a way of competing with men, rather as a way of enabling women to do their social and moral 'duties' better. Reason would not only keep wanton emotions and instincts in check but will further allow women to have self-mastery and psychological independence. Considering Wollstonecraft's family tragedies, she considered them to be essential skills for girls to learn so that they would not be overwhelmed by personal difficulties.

The book included useful guidance on topics ranging from 'Moral Discipline', 'Artificial Manners', 'The Benefits Which Arise From Disappointments' to acute observations on 'Boarding-Schools', 'The Observance of Sunday' and 'On the Treatment of Servants'. She critiqued the wasteful and frivolous pastimes women occupied themselves with, leading to their own intellectual and moral decrepitude. To a great extent, Wollestonecraft's inputs came from a particularly painful period when she worked as a governess for the family of Lord and Lady Kingsborough. The latter personified all that Wollstonecraft found wrong with women's education—such ladies not only led intellectually desiccated lives but were primed to exploit and belittle any woman—like Wollstonecraft herself who wanted to aspire for more.

Wollestonecraft was saved from economic misery by Johnson who invited her to work as a translator at his publishing house in London. The resulting financial independence gave wings to her intellect and she began writing on the dangers of inferior education of girls across genres. She had already written *Mary: A Fiction* when living in Ireland with the Kingsboroughs and now finished *Original Stories from Real Life; with Conversations, calculated to Regulate the Affections, and Form the Mind to Truth and Goodness* (1788). She also began writing, *The Cave of Fancy: A Tale* but could never complete it. She also compiled an anthology, *The Female Reader; Miscellaneous Pieces in Prose and Verse; Selected from the Best Writers and Disposed under Proper Heads; for the Improvement of Young Women* (1789).

POLITICAL WRITINGS

As part of her professional writing, Wollstonecraft translated into English several writings from the continent like Jacques Necker's *Of the Importance of Religious Opinions* (1788) from French, Rev. C. G. Salzmann's *Elements of Morality, for the Use of Children; with an Introductory Address to Parents* (1790) from German, and Madame de Cambon's *Young Grandison* (1790) from Dutch. Working for Johnson's radical journal *Analytical Review*, Wollstonecraft began writing commentaries on a range of topics, including history, politics, ethics and morality. This signalled the beginning of her direct engagement with political matters, and among the first of her works was a review of a speech made by her old friend, Revered Price, named, *A Discourse on the Love of our Country*. The speech had led the influential philosopher Edmund Burke to respond with *Reflections on the Revolution in France, and on the Proceedings in Certain Societies in London Relative to that Event* (1790) in which he not only advocated a status quo in society but also criticized English dissidents like Price for being swayed by thoughts of a foreign revolution.

RIGHTS OF MEN

Wollstonecraft responded to the attack made on the aged Revered Price by composing *A Vindication of the Rights of Men*. Though it first appeared anonymously in November 1790, the second edition that appeared a month later publicized Wollstonecraft as the writer and led to her recognition as a political and moral philosopher of significance. In the work, Wollstonecraft, like Price, disagreed with Burke's defence of institutions like Royalty and Church in France as well as the numerous links of family, community and tradition that gave a society its national character, and hence, had to be preserved. Instead, Wollstonecraft agreed with Price in believing that the rule of law, government and human relations could be simplified and understood in the context of freedom and equality. Though she agreed that freedom also entailed certain duties, in her mind she was clear that unless a person's natural rights were safeguarded, he could not be expected to fulfil his duties by society, country and God.

What is most interesting in *A Vindication of the Rights of Men* is how Wollstonecraft expanded the scope of the political to include the institution of family and women's condition as well. While Price, in his speech, had criticized men of authority for their moral and sexual licentiousness, Wollstonecraft in her *Vindication* went further and brought the blame squarely at the door of the institution of family, in particular, and society, in general. She argued that society was only concerned with the acquisition of wealth, and would regulate marriages and arrange them as thinly masked business deals. For men to become morally reformed, it was necessary to begin with the family which, fundamentally, meant that there was a need to bring about reforms for female education. Bringing up girls without learning or skill mediated by Reason meant that all they learned was coquetry and vanity, which, eventually, led to the moral and political degradation of the entire society.

RIGHTS OF WOMEN

The depth of Wollstonecraft's convictions became clear when within a few months of the publication of *A Vindication of Rights of Men*, she wrote and published her iconic text, *A Vindication of the Rights of Women* in 1790. The book continued her deeply felt concerns about the way girls were brought up at the time—kept busy in pointless activities like needlework at best and in flirtatious pursuits at worst—instead of developing their rational and practical skills which would help them to take care of themselves as well as their families in the most productive way. True education meant an improvement of women's physical and mental faculties, based on Reason and towards a life of virtue. Just like the rights of man were written in response to Burke's defence of traditional ways of life in the *Reflections on the Revolution, the Rights of Women* was also directed at the gendered, stereotypical thinking of yet another highly influential philosopher of the times, Rousseau.

In *Emile*, Rousseau made a passionate argument to return to a system of education grounded in the natural way of life; but this project had, at its heart, was the male subject, with women figuring mainly as educational aids furthering the cause of the male learner. Wollstonecraft bitterly attacked this excessive concern with feeling and sensibility, besides taking issue with the sidelining of women's interests for the sake of men's education.

She strongly believed that Reason was the best guide to bring about a moral and social betterment, both for men and women. And to this effect, she outlined several educational reforms, ranging from changes in the existing school curriculum to demands for women to learn midwifery, nursing, even medical sciences to combat the appropriation of these areas by men. More importantly, she exhorted the need for women to learn practical and employable skills which would help them become financially independent in case of widowhood they remained a spinster. At the same time, she gave tips on saving marriages, suggesting that the choice of a life partner should be based on mutual friendship and respect rather than on physical attraction. Wollstonecraft's demands for wider reforms included civil rights for women as well as political representation for the ultimate benefit of the society as a whole. In her book, more than ever, she argued the case for women to be strong and independent—for them to seek self-worth not in their outward appearance and male admiration but in the sense of self-mastery and self-realization within.

PERSONAL CRISIS

For all Wollstonecraft's advocacy of Reason, there came a time in her own life when the heart overruled the head. Wollstonecraft became romantically involved with American writer Gilbert Imlay and also had a daughter out of wedlock. Soon though, the couple grew apart and Wollstonecraft twice attempted suicide. The torturous times found expression in *Letters from Sweden* (1796) that she wrote during a tour of Scandinavia where she contrasted the misery within her to the beauteous surroundings around, thereby imbuing and enhancing travel literature of the times with an important tenet of Romantic movement. In these letters, the strident rationalism of the rights of women was much softened as the writer struggled with the twin pulls of desire and reason, dependence and autonomy.

The complexity of the *Letters from Sweden* caught the attention of William Godwin, another writer of the radical group during the times of Johnson. Godwin and Wollstonecraft grew close and upon discovering that she was with child, the two got married.

The tumult in her personal life would lead to her final work, *The Wrongs of a Woman, or Maria*. In this work, Wollstonecraft gave voice to two women from opposing ends of the social spectrum—one, a prostitute and the other, the wife of an upper-class man—who narrate the miseries that they undergo because of economic and social dependence on men and the legal support of patriarchy. The thinly-veiled fictional device was used by Wollstonecraft to make a case for equal companionship, economic and sexual freedom for women so that they could lead their lives with independence and dignity.

DEATH AND LEGACY

Ten days after the birth of her daughter, Wollstonecraft died; she was only 38. Upon the publication of her last novel as well as her biography by Godwin, Wollstonecraft's reputation came under a cloud. The revelation that she had not been married during the birth of her first child and details of her relationships with married men led to the side-lining of her contribution to the nineteenth-century movement for women's reforms. However, her personal legacy would survive in the form of her second daughter, also named Mary, who would go on to author the hugely popular novel, *Frankenstein*—a parable of the horrors that ensue when something is created only out of greed and without love or responsibility. This work would directly relate to her political concerns including the need for freedom for men and women.

Only after when the prudery of the Victorian Age had

passed, that feminists in England and the United States acknowledged the value of Wollstonecraft's vision of rational, economically and sexually independent womanhood. In her recognition of the emotional and sexual needs of women, while demanding economic and social independence, Wollstonecraft anticipated many of the dilemmas of modern-day feminists. Finally, in her assertion that it was only through including women's intellectual and economic empowerment that true social progress could be brought about, Wollstonecraft made the first connection between the political and personal that would go on to underline the women's liberation movement in the twentieth century.

«KNOW MORE»

- As a girl, Wollstonecraft would sleep in front of her mother's bedroom door to prevent her father from beating her mother.
- Famous Romantic poet William Blake illustrated Wollstonecraft's *Original Stories from Real Life*, with his engravings.

16

THOMAS JEFFERSON

Thomas Jefferson was one of the Founding Fathers of the Constitution of the United States and the principal creator of the American *Declaration of Independence*. He went on to become the country's third President, second Vice President and its first Secretary of State. Apart from being a politician, statesman and diplomat, Jefferson left his mark as an intellectual and political writer in his presidential messages, addresses, the declaration as well as numerous public papers, bills, letters and his sole book, *Notes on the State of Virginia*.

EARLY LIFE

Born in April 1743 at Shadwell in Virginia, Thomas Jefferson grew up in a family that had benefited as much from a lineage as from self-improvement. While his mother was a descendent of one of the oldest and well-established families of Virginia, his father was a self-made farmer and surveyor. After the latter's death in 1757, young Jefferson moved out of the family home to first live with the local schoolmaster Rev James Maury and then attended the William and Mary College in Williamsburg. There, Jefferson met thinkers and writers engaged in passionate discussions about politics, law, economy and, especially, the condition of American states as British colonies—all of which fashioned his future career as a lawyer and politician.

After leaving college, Jefferson began to practice law, but his innate political ambitions led him to enter the House of Burgess. His political timing was astute, as the early 1770s were marked by increasing opposition to the exploitive British policies in the American colonies. Jefferson was a passionate advocate of American freedom and this was amply expressed in *A Summary View of the Rights of British America* that he wrote in 1774, which went on to be published without his permission. Nevertheless, the impact of the paper was considerable and it established Jefferson's reputation as a political thinker. In this work, he clearly pointed out that American people were related to Great Britain not out of any political or moral subjecthood but only because of voluntary loyalty to the king.

EARLY CAREER

Jefferson was elected to the Continental Congress in 1775 and thereafter, was invited to be part of a committee tasked with drafting a formal statement of reason justifying a break with Great Britain. For two weeks, he worked at it and the result was the *Declaration of Independence* that was approved on 4

July 1776. This contained the essence of Jefferson's political philosophy according to which, all men were created equal and possessed inherent rights of life, liberty and pursuit of happiness. Equally important, the declaration also included the right to revolution, which entailed the right of the governed in case of long periods of exploitation to pull down any tyrannical form of government. In order to put these ideas in action, Jefferson, after his return to Virginia, started a series of legal reforms. These included abolishing laws such as of primogeniture, entailment and others which prevented the broad distribution of property, opening up educational opportunities for all, and finally, complete separation of the Church and State. Together, these reforms made up the kernel of his political vision that was to be expressed fully in the years to come.

REPUBLICANISM

The *Declaration of Independence* clearly stated that the governments owed their origin to the governed and derived their powers from the consent of the people. Any form of political system that took its power from birth or lineage was an anathema to him. This would form the crux of Jefferson's model of Republicanism, which is expressed in his political activities and writings after his return from France in 1789. During his tenure as the secretary of state and then as the vice president, Jefferson opposed a centralized federalist structure of the American government. He was wary of a strong aristocratic group of wealthy merchants and bankers consolidating power in their own hands. He feared this would lead to the neglect and exploitation of the wider American society, especially those who lived off the land.

However, with Jefferson winning the hotly-contested presidential elections of 1800, he struck a more conciliatory note in his Inaugural address with his now famous line, 'We are all Republicans...we are all federalists'. Even then he made it clear that the government took its source of power from the voluntary will of the people which is expressed through elections, and it should guide the decisions made by and the direction of the republic. During his presidency, he reduced the size of the federal government and limited the scope of its activities. He also paid off the government's debt while putting an end to internal taxes. Reducing the size of the federal army and navy was yet another measure in limiting the federal powers of the republican government.

SECOND PRESIDENCY

Though during his presidency, Jefferson rarely took unilateral federal decisions, those that he did were also his boldest. An example was the Louisiana Purchase of 1803 which firstly, removed the threat of the French presence from America's borders. Secondly, it threw open the Western frontier to put into action Jefferson's cherished republican ideal of agrarian living. Not surprisingly in the elections next year, Jefferson was re-elected for a second presidential term. However, certain domestic measures like the Embargo Act of 1870 and international conditions, like loss of trade due to Napoleonic

Wars, led to a decline in his popularity. Thus, by the end of his second presidential term, he was relieved to give up his office and head to retired life.

OTHER WRITINGS

In the last decades of his life, Jefferson wrote a great deal, especially letters to other thinkers, politicians, philosophers and friends in which he continued to refine his definition of republicanism. One such letter to DuPont de Nemours, dated 24 April 1816, listed nine 'moral principles' which, according to Jefferson, made up the foundations of republican government. Of these nine, the seventh stated that 'Action by the citizens in person, in affairs within their reach and competence, and in all others by representatives, chosen immediately, and removable by themselves, constitutes the essence of a republic'. Among other principles that he believed were crucial to safeguard the republic was the freedom of religion and the freedom of the press.

Jefferson's most famous correspondence during this time was with his former friend and later presidential opponent, John Adams. During their political careers, the two had grown apart to represent two opposing impulses of the American Revolution. Jefferson stood for a clean break with the past and rejection of federal imposition on civil liberties. Adams, on the other hand, symbolized the connection with the 'motherland' and recognition of institutions like the colonial assemblies that had, eventually, helped America become free. The letters of these later years are marked by some sort of recognition of how their opposing stances actually stood as for a metaphor of the inherent pulls in the American Republic.

Jefferson's republicanism was both democratic and meritocratic—the former as it was founded on the equality of men and the latter because he also recognized natural differences among men in their capabilities and qualities. This would become the basis of his concept of 'natural aristoi'—an aristocracy based on virtue and talents rather than on the artificial aristocracy founded on birth and privilege. According to Jefferson, in an ideal state, public offices, as well as professions like teaching and scientific research, were best held by men from the natural aristocracy.

CONCEPT OF CONSTITUTIONAL RENEWAL

In the final analysis, Jefferson's understanding of republic went further than any other political structure. Indeed, it was not meant to be understood as a particular system of governing at all, rather a template in which the will of the people was above all. For this reason, too, Jefferson clarified that a government should not be shackled to a particular constitution since the latter was just a provisional representation of the will of the people at the time of its drafting. This led to his belief in periodic constitutional renewal in order to keep up with the political and social progress of the country. The concept was itself based on the theory of 'usufruct', according to which the dead neither have rights nor powers over living people and hence, the latter should not be bound to laws laid down by the former.

Despite the firm belief in the government's 'absolute acquiescence in the decisions of the majority', Jefferson was clear from the very beginning of his presidency that no majoritarian argument could be used to override civil liberties, including rights of minority groups. In his 1801 inaugural address, he clarified that 'though the will of the majority is in all cases to prevail, that will, to be rightful, must be reasonable; that the minority possess their equal rights, which equal laws must protect, and to violate would be oppression.'

DEATH

The last seventeen years of Jefferson's retirement were spent in writing, corresponding with and meeting visitors who gravitated towards his mansion Monticello for a chance to interact with the famous statesman. There was also the large family of his daughter Martha—extending to twelve grandchildren—that kept Jefferson happily engaged in the final years of his life. But such a hectic social life also meant that Jefferson incurred huge expenses and was heavily in debt towards the end of his life. He breathed his last on 4 July 1826 on the golden anniversary of his beloved country's independence.

Apart from the huge mountain of debt that he left behind—which resulted in his daughter Martha losing the family home—Jefferson's reputation, later, came under a darker shadow owing to his ambiguous position on slavery. Despite asserting that all men were created equal in the *Declaration*, he owned slaves all his life, and during the debate over the Missouri Compromise in 1819, he even supported the expansion of slavery across the western territories. Likewise, his project of western agricultural expansion refused to take into account the position of Native American tribes who had lived and hunted there for centuries.

LEGACY

Despite such contradictions, Jefferson's vision of a free and equal society inspired many subjugated people in Asia and Africa to throw off their colonial yoke. The most popular passage from the *Declaration of Independence* continues to resonate with democracies all over the world.

We hold these truths to be self-evident; that all men are created equal; that they are endowed by their Creator with certain inalienable rights; that among these are life, liberty and the pursuit of happiness; that to secure these rights, governments are instituted among men, deriving their just powers from the consent of the governed.

Though Jefferson never wrote a formal political treatise in his life, the essence of his political philosophy lay in his passionate advocacy of republicanism. Being a government of and for the people meant that republicanism allowed the participation of the maximum number of people in civic life. Even more importantly, according to Jefferson, this was the only system that helped everyone to realize their human potential to the fullest. Over the course of human history, political elites based on hereditary privilege had denied massive numbers of people not only equality but also liberty to be the best they could. Allowing people equality before the law and equal access to opportunities meant granting people freedom in the truest sense, so that they could fulfil their dreams and potential. This, for Jefferson, proved that republicanism was the most progressive among all forms of government.

«KNOW MORE»

- Thomas Jefferson was a firm believer in the benefits of waking up early to begin his day. Among the first things he did in the morning was bathing his feet in cold water.
- He spoke six languages, including English, French, Greek, Italian, Latin and Spanish. He wrote more than 19,000 letters over his lifetime.

17

JOHN STUART MILL

John Stuart Mill was a nineteenth-century British philosopher and intellectual who is best remembered today for the development of Utilitarianism and his powerful defence of liberty. His theories on ethics, as well as moral, political and economic philosophy, defined Victorian era reforms and progress in significant ways.

EARLY LIFE

Born on 20 May 1806 at Pentonville, the family home of James Mill in London, young John grew up under the exclusive intellectual guidance of his philosopher-economist father. By the age of ten, John had already read the works of classical authors like Plato, Demosthenes, Diogenes, Xenophon, Lucian, Isocrates—in the original, besides studying algebra, Euclid's geometry as well as a good deal of English history—an achievement that was usual for the much older university students. Soon, young Mill familiarized himself with the political economy of Adam Smith as well as the writings of English economist David Ricardo and pursued his interest in scholastic logic as well as Aristotle's ethical treatises. In his youth, a year spent with the Bentham family as well as studies in varied subjects such as botany, chemistry, psychology and mathematics added to his preparations for a life of intellectual and philosophical inquiry.

Much has been written about the academic rigour and intellectual discipline that young Mill had been subjected to during his childhood by his father. Such a strict environment undoubtedly led to Mill's stern outlook towards life, and perhaps, developed into a mental strain. Nevertheless, the early grounding in academics helped Mill to learn the fundamentals of logical inquiry which involved confronting a problem, collecting and weighing evidence in favour or against a solution. Additionally, habits of hard work, extensive reading and intellectual courage that he acquired in these early years would prove invaluable later on.

Despite James Mill earlier planning of a career in law for his eldest son, John secured an appointment with the examiner's office at the India House right after turning seventeen. In 1828, he finished his probation and from 1836 for the next twenty years, he remained at the helm of British East India Company's affairs in the Indian colony.

WRITINGS ON PHILOSOPHY

Secure in his appointment at the India House, Mill felt himself questioning many of the influences of his earlier life. Later in his autobiography, he would go on to describe this as a time of 'mental crisis'. He felt that this had been brought about by an excessively rigorous intellectual life and the consequential neglect of emotional life in his childhood. After reading Wordsworth, Mill felt himself becoming more receptive to poetic suggestion and developing emotional intelligence. Among the results of this new confidence was Mill's 1843 work titled *A System of Logic*, where he presented a critique of inductive logic, particularly pointing out the failings of syllogisms. Instead, Mill advocated the use of a form of logic derived from the principles of the natural sciences, thereby providing a solid, scientific methodology for reasoning and philosophy.

WRITINGS ON ECONOMY

Mill next turned his attention to the economy and wrote *Principles of Political Economy*, which was first published in 1848. It soon became one of the most widely read books on the subject and, in fact, was part of the curriculum at Oxford University till 1919. In this work, he advocated more equitable distribution of wealth in society, insisting that political economy could no longer perpetuate the outdated theory that bound maximum production with the greatest independence of productive agents. Towards this end, if necessary, Mill even supported the intervention of State despite his fundamental opposition to its influence outside governance matters.

DEFENCE OF LIBERTY

The need to adopt a more liberal outlook to mankind was spectacularly expressed in *On Liberty*—a powerful defence of the individual's moral and economic rights in the face of society, in general, and governments, in particular. Though Utilitarian Radicalism had seemed to establish the foundations of democratic freedom, the liberty of the individual was by no means a clearly defined principle. *On Liberty* marked Mill's success not only in doing that but in combining the principle of liberty with the limitations of social life into an organic whole.

In this work, Mill propounded his famous 'harm principle' according to which, the only justification for exercising power over a person in a civilized community is to prevent him/her from harming someone else. This principle was remarkable for its highly progressive implications—for one, it disqualified self-interest as sufficient reason for the use of power over another human being and secondly, it did away with paternalism. Mill believed that an individual should be allowed to decide what is right or wrong for him rather than the state or someone else assuming that authority. More importantly, he made a distinction between actions which harm others and those which might merely offend—thus removing objections and liberating opinions and expression. Above all, despite some vagaries in his arguments, later, pointed out by critics, Mill's *On Liberty* unequivocally upheld a person's freedom to live the way he/she wanted as well as its implications.

In 1861, came Mill's *Considerations on Representative*

Government in which he presented an eloquent and sustained defence of representative democracy, especially in comparison to benevolent despotism. This tract clearly laid down two essential traits of good governance—firstly, to promote the common good which was understood as both virtue and intelligence of the citizens, and secondly, to realize the potential of the people in service of the common good.

REFINING OF UTILITARIANISM

Also in 1861, Mill went back to one of his earliest philosophical theories—that of Utilitarianism. Influenced by Jeremy Bentham's concept of utility as well as by the writings on human motivation by psychologists such as Étienne Bonnot de Condillac and Claude-Adrien Helvétius, Mill had founded the Utilitarian Society as early as in 1822–23, when he was not even out of his teens. Mill's understanding of Utilitarianism was primarily shaped by the writings of Philosophical Radicals, to which both his father and mentor Jeremy Bentham belonged. According to them, two fundamental drives—the pursuit of pleasure and avoidance of pain—lay at the heart of all human motivation. Thus, the utility could be understood as that particular property in any object that sought to bring the two together.

Mill initially agreed with the general lines of Bentham's philosophy, including the concept that laws should be made to bring about the greatest good for the greatest number. Eventually, however, Mill began to give a more individual shape to his doctrine, proposing that it is not the quantity of pleasure that should be important to human beings—as had been stated by Bentham—but its quality exemplified by his famous quote, 'better to be Socrates dissatisfied than a fool satisfied'.

In this way, Mill countered the anti-utilitarians who objected that the philosophy promoted mere material or sensual pleasures. Mill, instead, was emphatic that the highest kind of 'utility' was the realization of imaginative, artistic and intellectual ideals. More importantly, the varied levels of utility was not a matter of subjective opinion because an intellect that aspired to a higher level of utility—personified by Socrates—had experienced both sides of the matter and was thus able to judge truly. Additionally, Mill also wanted his theory of utility to further human progress—rather than simply satisfy existing human desires. He was clear that the function of utility should be to fully realize the human potential in the path of improvement.

SUPPORT FOR SUFFRAGETTE

It was this deep concern with human progress that prompted Mill to support the movement for women's suffrage, in particular, and women's empowerment, in general. Though written in 1861, *The Subjection of Women* appeared in 1869 and contained one of the most pragmatic and forceful arguments in favour of equality of the sexes. He argued that every fully conscious being had the right to share in the government of all by all. Unjustly excluded for centuries, women must, he asserted, be granted voting rights.

Mill's writings on ethics, politics and philosophy created the foundations of a high-profile public life. After his retirement from the East India Company, Mill entered politics and was elected from Westminster as a Liberal MP in 1865. However, partly because of his support to many radical liberal causes like labour unions, easing of the financial burden on Ireland and abolition of slavery in the United States, he lost the second term. In 1873, he passed away in Avignon where he went regularly to visit his wife's grave; upon his own death, he was buried next to his wife.

LEGACY

Mill believed that the end purpose of a true system of political philosophy *was* 'to supply, not a set of model institutions but principles from which the institutions suitable to any given circumstances might be deduced'.

Though his own theory of Utilitarianism and refusal to extend his concept of Liberty to colonial subjects later came under criticism, his thoughts, nevertheless, left a lasting influence on ethical, political and economic institutions around the world. The core of his legacy contains powerful ideas expressed with brilliant lucidity and genuine concern for human progress, in the best traditions of the nineteenth century Age of Reform.

«KNOW MORE»

- Mill was the godfather of Bertrand Russell, a famous philosopher of the early twentieth century.
- In 1851, Mill married a woman named Harriet Taylor whom he had first met twenty years back when she was the wife of a wholesale pharmacist. After two decades of a platonic relationship, Harriet's husband died, finally leaving her free to marry Mill. However, within seven years of being happily married, Mill lost his wife to consumption at the Hotel de l'Europe in Avignon, France, where he had taken her to recuperate. Sometime later, Mill bought a small white house in the same town and decorated it with the same furniture that was present in the hotel room where Harriet had breathed her last. Mill was motivated to defend women's suffragette after being inspired by Harriet's support for the cause.

18

TOCQUEVILLE

Alexis de Tocqueville was a French historian, political scientist and administrator whose thoughts on democracy ushered in great changes in the expectations of modern societies from their political institutions.

EARLY LIFE

Alexis de Tocqueville was born on 29 July 1805 in Paris into an ancient French aristocratic family whose origins could be traced as far back as the Battle of Hastings in 1099 CE. His great-grandfather, Chretien de Malersherbes, had been an influential and learned statesman during the eighteenth century France who had lost his life to the guillotine in the aftermath of the French Revolution, something that Tocqueville's own parents had narrowly avoided. Nevertheless, young Alexis grew up idolizing de Malersherbes and his advocacy of reforms into the former French autocratic regime. Because of his family's aristocratic connections, a public office seemed the natural choice of career for him, and he became an assistant magistrate in 1827.

POLITICAL ASPIRATIONS

Tocqueville was greatly affected by all the political churning of the time in France. He read up English history and writings of historians like Guizot who pointed out the inevitability of aristocratic privilege, making way for greater democracy in governance. In his explorations, Tocqueville found a like-minded companion in Gustave de Beaumont and the two decided to travel through America, Algeria and England. They even collaborated on many works based on political writings, and eventually, entered the French Parliament together.

However, the July Revolution of 1830 compelled Tocqueville to rethink his political trajectory. The Revolution replaced the Bourbon kings whose patronage Tocqueville's family had enjoyed with the 'citizen king' Louis Phillippe of Orleans. Tocqueville was, thus, wary of the new political dispensation and as a way out of this complexity, decided to leave for America with the ostensible reason of studying their prison reforms. While the decision may have been hastened by the political developments of July 1830, Tocqueville had, for some time, been interested in America's political systems. While early in his career, he had been looking at Britain's constitutional monarchy as an option that France could follow in its path to greater political liberalism, over time, Tocqueville began to find in American democracy a more suitable alternative for France.

WRITINGS ON AMERICA

In between 1831 and 1832, Tocqueville and Beaumont spent around nine months in America talking to intellectuals and administrators, studying institutions and taking notes. The most immediate result of their visit was the book *On the Penitentiary System in the United States and Its Application in France* (1833), which they wrote together. Then came Beaumont's study of America's racial relations in *Marie; or, Slavery in the United States* (1835), while Tocqueville, from 1835 to 1840, worked on a comprehensive study of the democratic government in America and its relationship to its people, religion, the economy as well as other institutions. The result was the first part of *Democracy in America* published in 1840 which won its author immediate fame as a historian and political thinker. The book was widely read in England, Belgium, Germany, Spain, Hungary, Denmark and Sweden, but attained the status of a virtual classic in the United States. More importantly, it brought about a rise in Tocqueville's professional and personal fortunes in France. He now acquired widespread regard in the aristocratic and intellectual circles of France with his acceptance into elite academic societies such as Legion of Honour, the Academy of Moral and Political Sciences as well as the French Academy. The newly acquired renown helped him realize his long-time political dreams and he entered the Chamber of Deputies in 1839 and even acted as an occasional adviser to the July Monarchy on important state matters.

In *Democracy in America*, Tocqueville hailed democracy

as the most representative form of the political system based on his famous theory of 'equality of conditions'. This, he believed, was the founding principle of modern life in the 'Christian universe'. In this sense, democracy not only stood for a political system but for an entire way of life. In America's case, the geography of the country, the religious origins of Puritanism, the culture of its people, its earliest laws and all such 'habits of the heart' created conditions for the growth of equality. Indeed, it was the moral and legislative rules emanating from Puritanism that helped Americans integrate the equality inherent in a democracy with individual rights. In this work, Tocqueville recognized the role of Puritans like John Winthrop who had shown that real 'freedom' meant the freedom to do only what was just. This ethical focus would not only orient democracy towards virtue but would also combat dangers such as materialism which Tocqueville believed a democratic society could be particularly vulnerable to.

ON DEMOCRACY

Another long term consequence of democracy pointed out by Tocqueville was excessive individualism. Differentiating this from selfishness, he foresaw democratic individualism leading to a withdrawal of citizens from the public into private life. This, in turn, could result in what he described in the first volume of the book as the 'tyranny of the majority' and in the second as 'soft despotism'. More insidious and, therefore, more dangerous than the despotism of the individual, this would replace real citizen participation in public institutions with mere theoretical abstractions or impersonal bureaucratic structures. The result would be the eventual loss of political and intellectual freedom of people themselves. In order to counter this, Tocqueville looked to the grass-root organizations and public associations in America which were actively involved in discussing and achieving economic, religious or political goals.

Though Tocqueville, more than his contemporaries like Mill, Guizot, Constant and Madison, was less optimistic about the ability of legal structures to combat the dangers of democracy, he nevertheless found in American society 'an image of democracy itself'. In America, he could see the modern democratic political system in action and thereby, understand the great democratic revolution playing out in contemporary Western civilization.

FRENCH POLITICAL UNREST

Tocqueville's concerns about the dangers of soft despotism actually had a closer relevance to what was happening in France. He witnessed the growing disenchantment of the ordinary French people with the very Liberals who had come to power with a promise of giving more freedom. Equally disheartening to Tocqueville was the apathy of the government to the worsening economic condition of the lower and middle class. In fact, Tocqueville even warned his fellow deputies about the rising resentment in the country in an important speech in 1848 and soon, what he predicted came true. The July monarchy was deposed, and the Second Republic was established in France in 1848.

In the uprising known as the June Days, as well as the constitutional conflict that followed, Tocqueville initially sided with the government against the socialist demands of the Parisian workers but gradually recognized the strength of the revolutionaries. Nevertheless, his political fortunes improved and in successive elections, he was elected as a conservative republican to the Constituent Assembly and went on to become its vice president in 1850. Under Louis Napoléon Bonaparte, nephew of the great French Emperor Napoleon Bonaparte, Tocqueville even served as the foreign minister from June to October 1849, during which his main achievement was to prevent France from overextending its foreign military involvement. Equally significant was his contribution, as a reporter of the constitutional revision committee, in averting a showdown between the executive and the legislature. Nevertheless, Louis Napoléon Bonaparte's determination to seize power led to a coup d'état whereupon, Tocqueville was imprisoned for some time. Disgusted with the ambition and corruption of people around him, Tocqueville, upon his release, refused to swear an oath of loyalty to Bonaparte and retired from active politics.

Removed from the daily stresses of public life, Tocqueville poured all his energy into composing his second major work titled, *The Old Regime and the Revolution,* which remained unfinished to the end. He also wrote an autobiographical record of his political career titled, *Souvenirs,* but it was the former which revived his reputation as a political historian and thinker of great acuity. In the book, he pointed out that the French Revolution had not destroyed class and social hierarchies in one stroke. Echoing the Preface to *Democracy in America*, which described the march of equality as a 'providential fact', he explained the socio-political churning in France which had been taking place over several centuries. The gradual erosion of royal and aristocratic privileges had eventually given way to more rights to the common people.

More significantly, in *The Old Regime,* Tocqueville tried to identify the social and political causes which made France as accepting of despotism as in the older, pre-revolution times. He compared this state of affairs to what happened in America. While the great revolution there had led to more sustained, vigorous democratic institutions, in France, it had resulted in the recent despotism of Bonaparte which he termed 'bureaucratic tyranny'. Though Tocqueville identified regions like Languedoc as being more successful in preserving democratic changes, for example, in their greater autonomy and resistance to governmental centralization—Tocqueville, in general, appeared to be less optimistic about democracy in France than in the Anglo-American world.

DEATH AND LEGACY

The pervading pessimism in the writings of Tocqueville's final years was lifted very briefly by the popularity that his works enjoyed in France. In 1858, he moved to Cannes to recuperate from a bout of illness but he never totally recovered and passed away in 1859.

Tocqueville's writings played a huge role in the understanding of America as a modern democracy and what it meant for the rest of Western civilization. More importantly, it contributed to a deeper understanding of democracy not as the classical institution of Aristotle, but as a modern political system which grew out of and, in turn, nurtured a particular way of life. Finally, his caution about the apathy and tyranny growing out of democracy was also proved right by various historical events ranging from the two World Wars to the rise of neo-imperialism in the twentieth century.

«KNOW MORE»

- Tocqueville was a sickly child, prone to bouts of nervous exhaustion and long periods of convalescence.
- His claim that the world will more readily accept a 'simple lie' than a 'complex truth' is among the most popular quotes on human behaviour.

19

KARL MARX

German philosopher and socialist thinker, Karl Marx propounded the revolutionary theory of the demise of capitalism and the birth of communism. His seminal works in this area were *Das Kapital* and *The Communist Manifesto* which went on to inspire new generations of leaders across the world, who were determined to bring in more equitable social, political and especially, economic systems.

EARLY LIFE

Born on 5 May 1818 in the Prussian town of Trier, Karl Marx grew up in an atmosphere of intellectual freedom and social activism. His father was a lawyer of Jewish origin who converted to Christianity in order to escape the increasing restrictions being imposed on the Jewish community at the time. Young Karl grew up hearing discussions on Kant and Voltaire and thus imbibed a passion towards social causes early on.

This continued as Karl was introduced to the philosophy

of G.W.F. Hegel in the University of Berlin and soon, he had become part of a students' political group known as 'Young Hegelians', which espoused revolutionary methods to overturn the traditional political and religious institutions. Though Marx earned a doctorate in 1841 from the University of Jena, his reputation as a radical closed the doors of the academia which made him turn to journalism. He became the editor of a liberal newspaper *Rheinische Zeitung*, but before long, it was shut down by the Prussian government and Marx had to escape to Paris.

POLITICAL WRITINGS

In the middle of the nineteenth century, Paris was the political heart of Europe and not surprisingly, Marx dove deep into its liberal currents. Here, he encountered Friedrich Hegel who would become his collaborator and lifelong friend. But eventually, Marx's ideas proved too radical even for Paris and he had to leave for Brussels. There, Marx was deeply influenced by the socialist thinker Moses Hess and resumed writing. *The German Ideology* and *Theses on Feuerbach* were the literary products of this time which were published only after his death. In the meantime, Marx began efforts to connect with the socialist thinkers across Europe and one of the results was the formation of the Communist League in England. In 1847, the League organized a meeting of its central committee in London which asked Marx and Engels to write a manifesto. The result was Marx's landmark book, *Manifest der Kommunistischen Partei* or *Manifesto of the*

Communist Party in which he elaborated on his political theory of dialectical materialism that would go on to become the ideological foundation of communism.

DIALECTICAL MATERIALISM

According to Marx, a study of the history of human society revealed a series of conflicts between opposing forces that he termed, 'thesis' and 'antithesis'. Out of this conflict came a 'synthesis' of forces that resulted in change. For example, out of the conflict between the nobility and the serfs in a feudal society, emerged the capitalist mode of production. Unlike Hegel who believed that the direction of this change was determined by ideas, Marx said that only a material force determined the result of such a change. For Marx, it was the material condition of a society that, in fact, gave rise to ideas which in turn took shape as its religion, art, philosophy and so on.

HISTORICAL MATERIALISM

In accordance with his theory of dialectical materialism, Marx traced human history over five phases, beginning with the primitive communal system, then the slave system, followed by the feudal system, the capitalist and then socialist which was yet to come. In each of these phases of conflict, one half was economically exploited and the other was the exploiter. However, the struggle led to massive changes every time. This formed the kernel of his doctrine of historical materialism according to which, the economic conflict between major social classes resulted in newer epochs in human history.

The first phase was marked by the absence of conflict since the production of goods at that time just about sufficed for people, and there was no surplus. The second phase of human history was characterized by conflict between slave owners and slaves but also resulted in larger agricultural production which, in turn, led to feudalism. This was marked by the conflict between the aristocrats and serfs but with the arrival of machinery and factory system during the Industrial Revolution, the change took the form of capitalism.

BIRTH OF SOCIALISM AND COMMUNISM

Capitalism again was prone to its own unique stresses. In this case, the conflict was between the *bourgeoisie* or the owners of the means of production and the *proletariat* or the labourers who work for a wage. And though labour was the source of all surplus value (profit), instead of being shared with labourers, it was appropriated by the capitalists and invested in more machinery. According to Marx, this shrinking employment of the proletariat weakened their purchasing power which, in turn, caused the additional goods produced by the higher stock of capital to remain unsold in the market, thus leading to economic cycles of depression.

Marx predicted that out of this conflict between the owners of capital and labour, which was inherent in capitalism, would emerge socialism. This again would unfold in two phases—firstly, as a 'dictatorship of the proletariat' in which all class differences would end and the workers would assume power; the second stage would see the establishment of a communal society functioning on the principle of 'from each according to his ability, to each according to his need.'

ALIENATION OF LABOUR

All these ideas were further elaborated in *Das Kapital* which Marx wrote in 1867. Additionally, the book was significant for its concept of the 'alienation of labour' which, according to him, was among the worst effects of capitalism. Capitalism not only appropriated the surplus produced by the worker with his labour but also resulted in piecework, specialization and setting up of large industries. Together, all this led to a system that encouraged a fetish for products, harmful to both the labourer and consumer.

Most significantly, *Das Kapital* unfolded a further sophistication of Marx's concept of historical materialism. In this work, he related the economic foundations of society to its corresponding legal, social, political and religious institutions which maintain and perpetuate the former. Thus, he claimed that the political, legal, social relations that people establish were determined by the existing mode of production and mutual material relations. In Marxist thought, the process of production became the determining factor of social evolution, including its government, laws, morality, religion, family, traditions, art and philosophy. This central concept underlines the entire corpus of Marxist ideology from his own writings to those of the current thinkers.

ON RELIGION

Marx famously wrote in the introduction to *Critique of Hegel's Philosophy of the Right* (1843) that religion was the 'opium of the people' meaning that for millennia, it had been used by ruling classes to keep the working classes in a stupor of ignorance so that they did not rise up in revolt and fight for their rights. His stand on religion had a major impact on later Marxist and Communist leaders to the extent that USSR after Lenin and China under Mao Zedong adopted the policy of state atheism.

Marx's opposition to religion would soon be expressed in different ways in other ethical and human philosophies. Nietzsche, a later contemporary, would declare among his pithy aphorisms, 'God is dead'. This marked a dominant concern of Nietzsche's philosophical works—the end of the relevance of Christianity and its fundamental concepts in contemporary times. In *Beyond Good and Evil, Prelude to a Philosophy of the Future* written in 1886 as well as *On the Genealogy of Morals, A Polemic* in 1887, Nietzsche put forward reasons for his rejection of essential Christian precepts of good, evil, guilt, free will, conscience, vengeance, anger, punishment, altruism and so on. In place of these, Judaeo-Christian concepts borne out of weakness, resentment and revenge, he posited values associated with strength, creativity, self-confidence and self-mastery—the qualities of the 'superhuman'.

Thus, for both Marx and Nietzsche, freedom was the highest goal, though the ways to achieve it were different. While Nietzsche claimed that this freedom could be achieved by rising above slave morality and achieving self-mastery, Marx claimed that personal freedom was only possible with the dismantling of the class system.

DEATH AND LEGACY

Despite his enormous influence on later thinkers, Marx struggled to find acceptance in his own time. Apart from a ten-year stint in the United States with the *New York Daily Tribune* as a correspondent, he never could live for a long time at any one place. Because of the radical nature of his writings, he was asked to leave by the governments of Belgium, France and Prussia. He went back to London and though the British government never granted him citizenship, where Marx lived until his death on 14 March 1883.

'Marxist philosophy is like great poetry—after it, no one else can write without taking it into account', wrote the iconic Modernist poet, T. S. Eliot.

Marx's influence on the history of the world can hardly be overstated. Though others like Friedrich Engels and Moses Hess also put forward socialist ideas, it was Marx who formulated them into a coherent ideology. 'Workers of the World Unite', the last line of *The Communist Manifesto* and the epitaph on his grave would become the clarion call to overthrow exploitive and oppressive social, political and economic systems in Russia, China and in many other countries across the globe; and even in liberal democracies, socialism would eventually drive the State to more equitable institutions in society.

«KNOW MORE»

- For all his aversion to the ruling class, Marx married a woman of aristocratic lineage. She introduced him to Shakespeare, and he was promptly taken up by the Bard's works. His influence was seen in Marx's own writings whose prose style was epic and theatrical, often lending to impressive quotes.
- In his adulthood, Marx was afflicted with a debilitating skin disease, which later historians and biographers surmise, may have intensified his sense of 'alienation'.

20

MICHEL FOUCAULT

Michel Foucault was a French historian and philosopher whose writings on power and society had a profound impact on a wide range of social and behavioural sciences. His major works, *Sex, Power and Identity* as well as *Discipline and Punish* went on to influence new areas of Post-Structuralist and Feminist studies.

EARLY LIFE

Born as Paul-Michel Foucault on 15 October 1926 in the French city of Poitiers, the future thinker grew up in a conventional bourgeoisie family headed by a physician father. As Paul grew into a young adult, his brilliant and sometimes, eccentric mind made him want to leave the confines of his provincial upbringing and head towards the centres of academic innovation.

Thus, in 1946, when he was only twenty, he started studying at the Ecole Normale Superieure in Paris. Here, he was exposed to the newest research on philosophy and psychology and was even influenced by communism for a brief while. He graduated in 1952 but after teaching at the University of Lille for some time, he took on a series of positions that took him across Europe from Sweden to Warsaw and then Hamburg. In 1961, Foucault returned to Paris to defend his doctoral thesis titled, 'Madness and Unreason: A History of Madness in the Classical Age', which would be condensed and published in English four years later as *Madness and Civilization: A History of Insanity in the Age of Reason* in 1965. The work was one of his earliest treatments of the ways in which human society uses institutions to exercise power—in this case, using religion and later science, specifically psychiatry, to control by changing the definition and treatment of madness. Despite its brilliance, the book did not extend his recognition as a highly original thinker beyond close academic circles.

POLITICAL CONCEPTS

However, all that changed in 1966 with the publication of *The Order of Things,* in which, for the first time, he made the study of discourse as important as that of institutions down the ages. According to Foucault, every age had its own schemes of knowledge that he called 'epistemes' or 'discursive regimes,' which strictly controlled the limits of what could be thought and said by people in that society. Thus, discourse in this sense meant more than 'ways of thinking and producing meaning' and actually involved 'a form of power'. Towards the end of the book, he indicated two different directions to his future analyses—the critical and the genealogical. The former would include his study of the historical formation of systems of exclusion while the latter would expose the link between systems of exclusion and the formation of discourses. And though the use of the world 'genealogical' could be traced back to Nietzsche, it is this second method used as a conscious inquiry that marked Foucault as one of the most original thinkers in the history of Western philosophy.

The use of discourse in Foucault's works acquired a more political shape 1970s onwards. He showed that the emerging nation-states of seventeenth and eighteenth century Europe developed certain social institutions and practices that were needed at that time to optimize the productivity of its citizens. This resulted in the creation of the concept of 'man' who rather than being the immutable self of Renaissance times, could now be both physically and mentally re-formed. This led governments to come up with disciplinary technologies like prisons and mental asylums which, in collaboration with systems of knowledge like politics and psychiatry, could keep its people under scrutiny and thereby control them. So, if earlier he had traced the history of insanity, in 1977, with the publication of *Discipline and Punish: The Birth of the Prison*, Foucault outlined the history of punishment as a form of discipline. Discipline in this sense was symbolized by the nineteenth-century reformer Jeremy Bentham's Panopticon—a circular prison designed to keep each inmate in the sight of a central watchtower–and in contemporary society, by the surveillance camera.

BIO-POLITICS

However, the concept with the most political impact was that of bio-politics. According to Foucault, one of the most significant shifts in the history of Western political systems was from the way monarchical states of the past controlled its subjects by physical coercion to the practice of modern welfare state that used more indirect forms of social surveillance and process of 'normalization' to control its citizens.

The underlying sensibility of this practice of the modern welfare state was medical. Governments began to think that its citizens would be more productive for the state if specific measures were taken like reducing the population, widening the tax base and ensuring a steady supply of soldiers. The state found it easy to do all this by using disciplinary mechanisms to intervene in the lives of its people. Of such mechanisms, the medical institution turned out to be most effective as it allowed the state to directly monitor and intervene in the health of the population.

Soon, governments and similar institutions began to examine everything from social organization to sexual behaviour to not only define what was healthy, and normal but also to identify what they thought was unhealthy and deviant. Unlike the past, modern governments were less interested in eradicating the non-conformists, and more in keeping them in check. This comprised Foucault's notion of bio-politics and according to him, constituted the dominant trait of how the modern welfare state controlled its population. However, he also noted that even the modern state did not entirely abdicate use of coercive power. In times of breakdown of discipline or mass uprisings in the population, the state went back to the use of brute force to exercise control, especially of all that lay outside its borders.

STUDY OF POWER

The other significant concept that Foucault explained in his workings of state control was power. Opposed to the beliefs of the Age of Enlightenment, he argued that no system of knowledge treated its subject completely objectively—they were always invested with the dynamics of power. And yet, unlike later materialists, he also revealed that knowledge did not work as a mere tool of powerful people and institutions. Rather, the interplay of knowledge and power always took place in historically specific circumstances, leading to complex dynamics that he termed, 'power-knowledge'.

A fuller account of power was given in *The Will to Knowledge*, the first volume of *History of Sexuality*, which revealed how sex was the most intense site at which discipline and bio-politics intersected. If the state had to intervene in its population, the most effective way would be to monitor, regulate and control its sexual practices.

In *The Will to Knowledge*, Foucault showed that power and knowledge had never existed without the other and neither had any causal precedence over the other. Also, power was not the reserve of select persons or institutions but rather unfolded through inter-relationships that existed in society. Power relations emerged out of people acting on others and then, making them act in turn. Apart from control, the other consequence of such power relations was 'subjectivation'. Foucault explained this as the shaping of individuals according to historically specific categories such as heroic or ordinary, normal or deviant, scholar or soldier and so on.

However, if power and 'subjectivation' made up one side of the coin, the other was resistance. To exercise one's power in making someone else do something implied that there was already resistance to it. In this way, for Foucault, resistance was not a later strategy to counter power but an in-built corollary in the exercise of power. By extension, even his theory of 'subjectivation' allowed for some space to lead to new practices of the self—a concept that he would elaborate in his study of ethics in the 1980s.

CONCEPT OF 'GOVERNMENTALITY'

By far, the closest Foucault came to engaging with themes of political philosophy in a series of lectures that he delivered over 1978 and 1979 titled, *Security, Territory, Population as well as The Birth of Bio-politics*. In the former, he introduced the concept of 'governmentality' that he explained as the logic used by states to govern its people. However, unlike the political philosophers of the Enlightenment, Foucault did not see this logic as ideal but as being made up of ideas, practices and institutions. He went on to define it as a complex form of 'power which has the population as its target, political economy as its major form of knowledge, and apparatuses of security as its essential technical instrument'.

Tracing the history of 'governmentality', he identified the first phase as that of *raison détat* or 'reason of state' marked by the overt use of police to discipline and control the society. Parallel to the shift he had noted in *Discipline and Punish*, Foucault identified the second phase of 'governmentality' from eighteenth century onwards when the failure of government control led to the belief that society should be allowed natural self-regulation. Also, the police should intervene only in extreme instances of disruption of order, and its power should be applied negatively. It is this stage of 'governmentality', marked by subtle entwining of individual freedom and population regulation that formed the subject of *The Birth of Biopolitics*. It is one that Foucault identified as working in contemporary times in the form of a political 'neo-liberalism.' Though Foucault never theorized 'governmentality' in as exacting a manner as he had done with regard to 'biopolitics', nevertheless, the former term expanded the latter in important ways—taking it further back into history as well as enlarging its scope to include elements like economics.

By the 1980s, Foucault gravitated towards a study of ethics from where he coined the word 'ethopoiein' to describe the process by which it was possible for an individual to transcend the limits of subjectivity and transform the self. Some scholars deciphered in this late concern with ethics and subjectivity as well as in his study of classical Ancient texts from Greece and Rome, a retreat from political project to individual action. But rather than withdrawal from his earlier theories, his new concern with subjectivity was yet another example of his method of building a central theme by adding layers of meaning. Just like he had done with the concept of power, he sought to create a new approach rather than agree or disagree with an existing one. Foucault explained subjectivity as the ability of individuals to shape their own conduct. This, in turn, related subjectivity to his previous ideas on government so that subjectivity could be understood as a way of governing one's own self. In this way, subjectivity was closely integrated to Foucault's political thought, as an expression of the power that permeated to the deepest layers of the individual.

DEATH AND LEGACY

Foucault's writings and lectures made him famous as a philosopher around the world. Apart from France, he visited Japan, Brazil, Canada, Italy and the United States to live and work. For many years, he taught at the University of California at Berkeley in the capacity of a visiting lecturer and during the same time, he contracted HIV and by the summer of 1983, he had to be admitted to a hospital in Paris. On 10 June 1984, Foucault died as a result of pulmonary complications arising out of AIDS-related septicaemia.

Foucault's influence on social and behavioural sciences has been extensive and complex. His critique of 'man' was labelled in some quarters of the academia as radically anti-humanist while other critics summed up his elaboration of power-knowledge as highly relativist. However, there is hardly any discipline which has not been touched by his understanding of the workings of discourse, its subtle links with power and its exercise through social institutions as a form of sociopolitical control. His critical history of ideas, modernity and institutions gave new directions to post-structuralism and post-modernism, besides revealing the necessity of multidisciplinary engagement in feminist, post-colonial, cultural, communication, sociological and anthropological studies as well as literary and critical theories.

Though Foucault did not contribute to political philosophy in the sense of normative politics, his ideas compelled political thinkers and policymakers to look at the relations between the state and its citizens anew. His treatment of themes like domination and 'subjectivation', discipline and bio politics opened up new vistas in the study of political science and allied subjects like law and governance. Most significantly, Foucault, by his on-ground support for many anti-government movements around the world, notably the Basque separatist, set a personal example of the importance of direct political action.

«KNOW MORE»

- Foucault's bent for originality extended to his personal style as well—he shaved his head and mostly dressed in black and white.
- Foucault drove a Jaguar; his favourite food was reportedly a turkey club sandwich and Coke—American staples that in contrast to fine French cuisine, he thought, exemplified simplicity and austerity.

CONCLUSION: NEW DIRECTIONS

A study of the history of political philosophy over twenty centuries clearly shows how crucial is the identity of a person as a citizen. It defines not only his or her rights, responsibilities and actions in the larger society but also impacts access to resources, relationships and overall quality of life. Political philosophers have, down the ages, tried to understand and theorize this relationship between the citizen as well as the State and its political institutions besides elaborating on what makes the Ideal State and how to achieve it. One only needs to read the constitutions of the most powerful countries to understand how deep and continuing has been the influence of these political philosophers.

However, since society itself is constantly changing across time and space, naturally, any study of its relationship to its citizens will also keep evolving. The same has been true of the study of political institutions to the extent that towards the end of the twentieth century, Foucault showed the impossibility of using the tradition of rational arguments to understand the truth about political institutions. This is because, according to him, each discourse is just another way to wield arbitrary power over others. Foucault's position led to the influence of post-modernism in political philosophy, marked by a newer understanding of how different ideologies down the ages have exercised and perpetuated political and economic power. Thus, feminism in the works of Kate Millet's *Sexual Politics* and Alison Jaggar's classic text, *Feminist Politics and Human Nature*, took up the subjugation of women in formal political institutions and began to explore the ways women could reclaim their rightful position in political life while post-colonialism feminists began to question the Eurocentrism of traditional concepts of political science.

The collapse of the communist bloc in the 1990s clearly shifted the focus in political studies from how different political ideologies and governments exercise power to the role of non-government space and civil society. Today, with the rise of identity politics and neo-imperialism, political philosophy faces typically worldwide concerns like the need for a global theory of justice to reduce the ever-widening gaps between developed and less-developed world, the prospect of global climate change, as well a threat of international terrorism and related issues like fundamentalism, refugee crises and displacement.